DOUBLE
LIVES

For Mum, you would have loved this one.

KATE McCAFFREY
DOUBLE LIVES

echo

echo

Echo Publishing
An imprint of Bonnier Books UK
4th Floor, Victoria House, Bloomsbury Square
London WC1B 4DA
www.echopublishing.com.au
www.bonnierbooks.co.uk

Echo Publishing acknowledges the traditional custodians of Country throughout Australia. We recognise their continuing connection to land, sea and waters. We pay our respects to Elders past and present.

This is a work of fiction. Names, characters, businesses, places, events, locales and incidents are either the products of the author's imagination or used in a fictitious manner. Any resemblance to actual persons, living or dead, or actual events is purely coincidental.

First published 2022

Printed and bound in Australia by Griffin Press

The paper this book is printed on is certified against the Forest Stewardship Council® Standards. Griffin Press holds chain of custody certification SGSHK-COC-005088. FSC® promotes environmentally responsible, socially beneficial and economically viable management of the world's forests.

Cover designer: Lisa White
Page design and typesetting by Shaun Jury
Editor: Rochelle Fernandez

Scripture quotations on pages 90, 91, 115, 127, 132, 159, 165, 166 and 235–36 are from The ESV® Bible (The Holy Bible, English Standard Version®), copyright © 2001 by Crossway, a publishing ministry of Good News Publishers. Used by permission. All rights reserved.

A catalogue entry for this book is available from the National Library of Australia

ISBN: 9781760687564 (paperback)
ISBN: 9781760687571 (ebook)

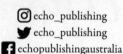

echo_publishing
echo_publishing
echopublishingaustralia

ABOUT THE AUTHOR

Kate McCaffrey is a Western Australian author who has published five Young Adult novels. She is currently touring schools, presenting workshops in Creative Writing, specifically for the Year 12 ATAR exam. Kate is also working in several different genres, from Contemporary Women's Fiction to Historical and Middle Grade Readers.

Kate lives on the northern beaches of Perth with her husband, daughters, two Maltese Shih-Tzus, and a cat called Not-Ruby.

CHAPTER 1
THE IDEA

The truth is in the detail. Within the nuance of the story, the cadence of the voice, the tilt of the head, the flutter of an eyelash. People are anthologies of stories, mosaics made up of minor events, small truths that constitute who we are, what we believe in, the way we live.

Why do I shake my head every time I'm offered a flute of champagne? Because, I'll laughingly tell my friends, I haven't touched champagne since the night I graduated from my Bachelor's degree and I drank so much I vomited out the back of my boyfriend's 1974 Ford Falcon. Of course, I believed I'd opened the door, but then I sheepishly acknowledge that I hadn't. And that admission, that self-awareness, that embarrassing truth, gives the story its required believability.

Before all of this began, I liked to think that I was a crusader for truth. It was a chalice brimming with indisputable goodness, the finding and the revelation of which would act as some form of emancipation from the other greatest defining feature of people: their secret.

Journalists are often regarded as creatures of prey. Great winged birds with curved beaks, who pick apart and rip through the meaty flesh of other people's lives. As a breed, we are viewed as toxic to privacy and secrecy. With our counterpart parasites, the photographers, we splash the front pages of magazines and newspapers with dark secrets that are often trussed up with pithy puns: a picture of Donald Trump's hair blowing in the wind captioned, 'There's gonna be hell toupee'; or President Bill Clinton's acquittal at his impeachment trial, 'Close, but no cigar'. These front pages give us what we creatures crave: money, success, greater opportunities. We march on, leaving a trail of carcasses in our wake.

I always held a higher moral ground – I'm not a print journalist, I write copy for radio shows. It is a widely held view in the industry that we are less exploitative, less tabloid and certainly more respectable. Our medium allows us to interview and record, and without the accompanying imagery – we all know a picture paints a thousand words – we can avoid the sensationalism that television and print are accused of.

Radio stations exist by genre. Christian radio punctuates

sermons and theological debate with up-beat tunes from Hillsong; the sports station relies on the commentators and laborious analysis of statistics on the field, on the track and in the pool – it's all about PBs and WRs. The alternative stations have it easier than most, unearthing new musical talent; trendy, hip doctors discussing physics and atoms; phone-in debates over the rights of cyclists on the roads. Alternative stations love on-air calls, interviews with politicians, online polls – we're always inviting text messages and comments on our website. Stations like Radio Western in Perth, where I work, offer listeners the opportunity to assist with the construction of the media we create and deliver. We allow consumers of media to be the producers of media.

I was looking for my big break, something that might resuscitate my sputtering career. Five years away from home, living and working in Melbourne, had given me experience in a small basement studio (listening audience of about two hundred – mostly friends and relatives), then a university-based station dealing with current and on-point issues, to my biggest gig ever: the presenter for the 2 a.m. to 5 a.m. time slot. You'd be surprised how many people are awake at that time.

Now, back in Perth, I was angling for drive time – a spot highly coveted by presenters. There's no greater captive audience, hemmed in by traffic for the ride home between

5 and 6 p.m. It's the jewel in the crown, the feather in the cap, or whatever accessory you'd like to pair with a head covering. Drive time was a radio journalist's nirvana.

Our competition – another alternative and millennial-loving station – had recently begun to use drive time for a cold-case exposé. Frankly, I found it a little too formulaic and highly unsatisfactory – after sifting through evidence and rehashing interviews, it still left listeners wondering whodunit. Apparently, the majority of the population disagreed with me and 44.3's ratings soared. They had well and truly hit it out of the park, scored a goal, made a touchdown – or whatever other sporting cliché you'd prefer. They were smashing us.

A council of war was called and we sat in the conference room for hour after hour, trying to be creative and innovative. How could we take it up to 44.3? Steal their listeners and crash their ratings? I did say radio journalists are only marginally more ethical than print ones. As the innovative concepts – or 'ridiculous, unsustainable tripe' (that was our producer Charlie's opinion) – were bandied about, it got me thinking.

***

It's 1917. Sydney is only 129 years old. King George V is the monarch and the prime minister is Billy Hughes, best known for two things – the first, leading Australia into the First World War and the second, for being the only prime minister to have served in politics for fifty years. The Town Hall is an ornate High Victorian Second Empire styled building that reflects the affluence and eager confidence of a booming city's population. The Town Hall's clock tower is the tallest structure in the city. The streets are wide on the official side of Sydney and lined with horses and buggies, businessmen in fedora hats and three-piece suits, women in high-necked, long-sleeved, ankle-grazing dresses – remnants of Queen Victoria's puritanical reign. The western side, meanwhile, reflects the convict days: the winding, haphazard roads, the rugged and rudimentary architecture, the work houses, the chimney sweeps and the labourers.

On the outskirts of this city, the charred remains of a woman are found. The victim is unidentifiable: her facial features destroyed, the large cracks in her skull evidence of her brutal and painful death. The case is unsolved. She is buried as a Jane Doe.

Harry Crawford is a short and stocky man who works odd jobs as a labourer, a meat worker and a bartender. Back in 1912, he was working as the driver for a doctor when he met the recently widowed Annie Birkett and her thirteen-year-old son, Harry Birkett. Crawford is persistent in his wooing of Annie, and she is receptive to his attentions; they marry in 1913. But the marriage is tumultuous. Crawford is a big drinker, and by 1917 the couple are often heard arguing. Neighbours report

Crawford has a temper and often smashes up the furniture in the house. In October of 1917 the couple go on a picnic to Lane Cove River. Annie never returns, and Crawford never reports her as missing to the police. Crawford tells her son Harry that Annie has left him for another man.

It isn't until 1920 that young Harry Birkett tells his aunt that on the day of his mother's disappearance, Crawford had taken Harry to the Gap, where they stood on the edge throwing stones. Harry, who never believed Crawford liked him, found his behaviour more unpleasant than usual. One night, about a week later, Crawford took Harry to an isolated area in scrubland and made him dig a hole, then they returned home. Suspicious, his aunt reports Crawford to the police. When the police search his house, where he lives with his current wife, Lizzie Allison, they discover a small bag. Crawford tells the police to open it, but not to allow his wife to see the contents. He says that in the bag is an artificial device that he has been using, which his wife doesn't know about. The police ask him if Annie knew about the device. To which Harry responds, 'Not until the latter part of our marriage.' The police arrest Harry on suspicion of Annie's disappearance.

The 1917 Jane Doe's remains are exhumed, and a gem found with her charred remains is identified by Annie's sister as belonging to Annie, and the false teeth are identified by the dentist as Annie Birkett's.

At the police station Crawford is charged with murder. They take his mug shot and fingerprint him, but before they can send him down, he states, 'I should be put in a women's ward.'

It was at this point that Harry's past, that of a woman, Eugenia Falleni, was revealed. Originally born in Italy, he had migrated to New Zealand as a child with his parents. Eugenia had dressed as a man from a young age, finding work on ships. At the age of nineteen he ran away to Australia; when he arrived in Sydney, he was pregnant, having been brutally raped by the ship's captain, who had discovered that Eugenia was transgender. He gave his daughter to a young Italian couple and set about creating his true identity, that of Harry Crawford, proceeding to live nearly all of his adult life as a man – until young Harry Birkett's revelation to his aunt.

As you can imagine, the press at the time went wild about what they called a 'he–she murderer'. To boot, in a society just liberated from the conservativism of Queen Victoria's reign, the 'instrument of pleasure' was actually submitted into evidence against Crawford at trial. Crawford was convicted of murder and sentenced to death. This was later commuted to life imprisonment. He was incarcerated for the rest of his life as a woman.

***

The story of Eugenia Falleni/Harry Crawford posed many questions for my investigative mind. Why did Harry murder Annie? Was it, as many speculated, that Annie had discovered Harry's past? By all accounts, Harry was a proficient lover; not only had he been married twice, but he also had female lovers on the side. If this was the case, did Harry kill Annie because of the attitudes towards homosexuality in those days? The notion of being transgender and the issues of sexuality raised by that weren't even a point of discussion at the time. Homosexuality alone would have ended in a prison sentence – what would have been the punishment for living transgender? Did Harry kill Annie because he was a violent and aggressive man? Because the society he lived in endorsed violence against women? Was it an accident? Had Annie, as Crawford always maintained, slipped and hit her head, dying instantly – after which he panicked, doused her in kerosene and set her body on fire?

It fascinated me, it perplexed me. I wanted to know the truth – but I was never going to get it from a case that was more than a hundred years old. There were no witnesses I could talk to, only dusty old transcripts that held one singular version of the truth, recorded in a moment in time.

I needed something modern, contemporary. I needed a case where the people were alive, the opinions current, the facts still able to be touched and examined. I wanted something that could make my listeners question what was at the heart of every person, their own identity.

I spent days poring over newspapers online, looking for that one story, the one with all the necessary ingredients. Murder, lies, deception, a dash of religion for good measure. Recently, I'd noticed that gender identity was getting more and more space in newspapers and magazines. The debate was being waged in schools and businesses. The terms transgender and non-binary are so familiar to us. But how accepting are we?

And then I found it. The Jonah Scott case.

At our weekly meeting I pitch my idea to Charlie and the team. 'Channel 44.3 are keeping their audience with intrigue, that we know, but there's nothing satisfying about it,' I say. 'A one-off pre-recording of a case that hasn't been solved and probably never will be. We want to find a case and turn it inside out. Look for the flaws, the mistakes, find the inconsistencies, seek the truth.'

'I'm not sure that's innovative.' Charlie looks bored. 'The ABC is following that formula with their documentaries.' Charlie is a bit of a mentor to me. As a high-school student I'd done some work experience with her, when she had run a small community station. We were friends on Facebook, and when I returned to Perth, Charlie offered me a job immediately. When I was desperate, when it felt like everything had imploded, she threw me a life-line. Her opinion means everything to me.

'My point exactly,' I say, getting excited. 'And it's working in that medium. Their ratings are monster, but I've got a twist. What say we make it up as we go along? Say, I do all the research over the next three months, get all the facts, create Episode One and then see what listener input we get? Like, we could actually get evidence from listeners that was never presented at the time. We could invite our listeners to help us discover the truth. I could then put together the next week's episode depending on where the first takes me.'

Charlie has straightened in her chair; she looks interested now. Her eyebrows have reached their apex. My colleagues are all leaning forward, there is a sudden charge in the air. 'So, when you start, you have no idea where you're going to end up?' she says. 'It could be risky.'

'Refreshing,' I say firmly. 'Imagine it, Charlie, presenting a show – an investigation, with no preconceived notion of the truth. Just a quest for the absolute. All I need is an assistant.' Charlie gives me that knowing look and then turns to our intern, Sarah.

'Do you want to be the lackey and general dogsbody?' she asks.

'Anything,' Sarah says. I can see she's hoping this will be her opportunity to make her mark in radio, as much as I hope it will be mine.

CHAPTER 2
I AM JONAH

'Hi, I'm Amy Rhinehart and I'm the presenter of *Strange Crime*, a live broadcast and podcast on Radio Western every Wednesday at 5 p.m. Season One is called *Double Lives* and examines the Jonah Scott murder of Casey Williams.

'Let me take you back to a summer night in mid-January. A girl's body is found floating in an isolated river in the state's remote south west. The Jane Doe, a victim of a savage stabbing attack, is unidentifiable. A manhunt begins, which leads detectives into a world of teenage sexuality, drug rings and religious cults, resulting in the conviction of then-nineteen-year-old Jonah Scott. The victim: his girlfriend Casey Williams. The outcome: Jonah's immediate confession and compliance with investigators. His plea: guilty. The sentence: life imprisonment.

'Sounds pretty straightforward, right? Boy kills girl, admits it, goes to prison. Probably the kind of case most detectives dream of. But what if, I don't know, something just doesn't add up? Something feels decidedly odd? Why go to such lengths – which we'll look at later – to cover up a crime, only to be totally compliant when the police show up? Why murder at all?

'I invite you all to tune in, every Wednesday, as I delve into the many parts of this case that don't add up. Oh, and listeners, we're doing this in real time. Each week we're producing one episode – this series isn't a pre-recording. We're going to see where this starts out and where we end up. So, I ask you to join me for the ride. Just a word of warning: listeners are advised that this podcast contains graphic and disturbing material.

'We begin Episode One, "I am Jonah", with part of the recording from our initial meeting with Jonah, back in March this year. My assistant Sarah and I travel to the maximum security prison about an hour out of the city. The drive is long. We pass through a razor-wire fence and pull up outside the main gate house. There are signs warning visitors about the consequences of bringing drugs in. We've been given special permission to bring in a recording device – but no photography is allowed. We sign in at the security check point. I have to admit I'm feeling nervous. Casuarina houses the state's worst and most violent criminals. Remember David Birnie? The serial killer who abducted, raped and tortured four girls in a killing spree with his wife, back in the 1980s? Yep, he used to live here, until his suicide in 2005. There is a tense atmosphere, I glance at the other visitors quickly, trying not to make eye contact as we sit in the waiting room.'

I press the button for the audio.

Guard: Rhinehart and Sutton for Scott. [Sound of gates opening, footsteps]

Amy [whispers]: We are now inside one of Australia's highest-security prisons. We're being shown into a non-contact room. It's divided by a glass panel. Jonah is tall, he has dark hair and a kind of gentle-looking face. His eyes are large and brown, he smiles at us with straight white teeth and gestures with one hand. He doesn't look at all like a murderer, and I'll explain what I mean by that in a bit.

Jonah: Hi.

Amy: Hey, I'm Amy and this is Sarah, we'd like to thank you for agreeing to participate in this series with us.

Jonah: Thank you for asking me.

13

Amy: We're curious, and I'm sure our listeners will be too, as to why you've agreed to be a part of our podcast.

Jonah: I'm confident in my relationship with God. But Casey wasn't, and now she's in hell. I was deceived and lied to. But it doesn't make what I did right. I took her life and I forced her into hell, because of who she was. I have a lot of time to think about that night. A night I wish I could go back to and do again, do again so differently. But God has a plan for me and this is it. He knows what He wants me to learn, to understand, inside these four walls, day after day. I pray to Him for forgiveness. I pray for redemption. But most of the time I pray for Casey. I pray that He can forgive her.

Amy: You've already been in prison two years. How has that changed you? How do you see yourself?

Jonah: I got sentenced to life imprisonment, with a non-parole period of twenty-three years. I'm twenty-one now, I was nineteen then, I could be forty-two when I'm released. I was a kid when I came in. I'd made a huge mistake. I was terrified. Who knows what the world will be like when I'm out? What technology will have done to us as people? How we'll live and love? I can't ever comprehend being outside these razor-wire fences, being free. And I know I don't deserve it. I gave up my right to freedom when I took Casey's life. But I really wish she hadn't lied to me.

Amy: What would you like our listeners to know about you?

Jonah: I've been portrayed as a brutal and violent killer, and I'm not that. I'm actually a good person. I'm loving and kind. I loved Casey. She had soft lips and gentle hands. I believe that in her heart she was good, too. I wish I could tell her that. When the cops arrested me, I knew I had to do the right thing. I had done something so bad, nothing was going to make that right. But my father said to me, 'Son, do the right thing now.' And that's what I did. I confessed and I pleaded guilty. No trial with jurors, just my admission and my punishment. But I know I'm yet to face my punishment, that remains between me and Him.

I pull my headphones back on. 'Before we plunge into the details of the case, I wanted you to hear the voice of the cold-blooded killer who stabbed Casey forty-seven times. Jonah then used a weapon to crush part of her skull, which would have rendered her dead instantaneously. He dragged her body to a wooded area near a secluded part of the river, where he tied a cement block to a rope. He pushed her body into the river – where it sank, and stayed for nearly three months.'

I pause. The violence of Casey's death is still so shocking

that I need to regain my composure. I look at my producer – she nods and indicates I have five minutes before the advertisement slot. 'Casey's body was discovered by a couple of hikers, and that led to the manhunt for Jonah. What makes this case the subject of this podcast is that there is something vital missing. Having gone to great lengths to dispose of her body and the murder weapons, Jonah confessed the crime instantly to the police. Not only that, but Jonah also pleaded guilty to the charge of murder, forfeiting his right to trial by jury.

'Now, stay with me here. On the recording you hear me say he doesn't look like a murderer. I know, right? What does a murderer even look like? The pictures I have of Jonah, before prison, show a young, gangly-looking boy – you know, your typical school photo, all teeth and long hair. The Jonah I met, the one you heard, is already a man. He is heavier set, muscly, I guess, his jaw is firmer. There is a hardness to his face.

'But that voice, you all heard it too, it's the soft and redemptive voice of someone seeking penitence. Jonah said he's a good person – loving and kind – and therein lies our conundrum. What on earth possesses a good person to stab someone forty-seven times and then bash their head in with a hammer? After the advertisement we'll be back to start picking this case apart.'

My producer is giving me a signal. I lift my headphones as I throw to the ads.

'Good start,' Charlie says, bringing me a glass of water. 'The text line is going mad. Listener numbers are spiking. When's the big reveal?'

'Next up.' I look at the monitor. I've got the hikers' discovery and the interview from the coroner cued to go. I go back on air.

'Thanks for staying with me. It was mid-January when two hikers, on their honeymoon, explored the forest down near the town of Nannup, some three-and-a-half hours from Perth. Please listen to this re-enactment.' I hit the button and the voice-over actress talks over haunting piano music.

Dusk was falling and the mist swirled gently across the river. In the reeds, insects and reptiles rustled for shelter. Birds flew en masse, circling and calling above the horizon as the damp air began to set in. The light, through the dense trees, changed momentarily to gold as the sun descended. The two hikers stopped and shifted their backpacks.

'It's getting dark.' Louis looked at his watch. 'We should probably get back before we lose all light.'

'I've got a torch.' Charlotte reached around into her pack. 'Here.' She flicked it on and cast it around the grove. Suddenly she shivered. 'You might be right, though. It's getting dark really quick, I don't want to be stuck out here tonight.'

They turned and followed the riverbank back the way they'd come, Charlotte's torchlight bouncing off the trees and reeds in front of them. A loud flapping noise across the surface of the river made her swing the torch nervously across it.

'It suddenly feels really creepy out here,' she said.

'Wait.' Louis held his hand up. 'Go back. What was that?'

'What?' Charlotte cast the torchlight across the river's blackness.

'That.' Louis grabbed her hand and steadied it on the shape in the water.

'A rock?' Charlotte said.

'No.' Louis took the torch, stepping closer. 'I don't think so. I think ...'

'Oh God –' Charlotte put her hand to her mouth. The light reflected the black water like an oil spill that pooled around the white and green mass floating on the surface of the water, revealing the faded pink singlet and the long brown hair that spread out like tendrils reaching, seeking, searching. 'It's a girl.'

'The couple called the local police, which led to the assembly of a Task Force, with detectives coming down from Perth. The small grove was lit up with high-powered lights as the police and detectives searched for clues, photographing and mapping any evidence they found.' I read from my monitor and glance at the clock. I have ten minutes left and I haven't played the coroner's report. I have to get it into the first episode.

'The body was dragged from the water, in a state of advanced decomposition. Now, listen to my interview with the current state coroner, Alistair Shaw.'

Amy: Welcome Alistair Shaw, thanks for being on the show. Can you tell our listeners what the role of the state coroner is?

Alistair: Sure. When a person dies from non-natural causes, it's my job to establish the manner in which the death arose, the cause of the death and the identity of the person.

Amy: What was the scene you were facing that day in January?

Alistair: Initially we had a young woman in her late teens to early twenties – age was difficult to ascertain at that point due to the extensive decomposition and insect activity.

Amy: Oh, yuck.

Alistair: Sorry, it is yuck, particularly bodies retrieved from water, which makes the identification of the person that much harder. It was clear at the scene of discovery that the person had been stabbed several times, and there was evidence of severe head trauma. In fact, it was one of the most confronting bodies I've ever had to examine in my entire career.

19

Amy: What else was noted initially?

Alistair: There was a long yellow rope tied securely around her waist. We ascertained that it had been attached to something heavy. Divers later retrieved a large cement building block from the bed of the river.

Amy: It was used to weigh her down?

Alistair: Yes. Given the time of year and the relatively warm currents, it would only have been a matter of days before a body thrown into the river surfaced again. Instead, because the body was tethered to the river floor, it, in fact, took three months from the killing to the discovery.

Amy: What was learnt at the autopsy?

Alistair: Once we had the body in the morgue, we conducted a complete autopsy. We discovered the forty-seven stab wounds had sliced or penetrated nearly every vital organ, there was evidence of mass haemorrhaging. Cause of death was the three blows to the skull, made by a claw hammer. The identity of the victim was difficult to determine.

Amy: Why was that?

Alistair: Firstly, we had no Missing Persons report that matched our victim's initial profile, and then at the autopsy

*it was revealed we'd been looking for the wrong
missing person.*

Amy: What do you mean by that?

*Alistair: Before the autopsy, the police were searching for
a record of a young woman between the ages of fifteen and
twenty-five, approximately 170 centimetres tall, about
fifty-eight kilos, long brown hair, pale blue eyes. Whereas
in fact they should have been looking for a young male, or a
transgender woman, of that description.*

Amy: Can you explain, please?

*Alistair: Yes, our autopsy revealed that our victim
was in fact a transgender woman. She had had breast
augmentation and showed signs of hormone therapy, as well
as retaining her penis.*

I look at Charlie, she's giving me the thumbs-up. The text line
has lit up. We've got our hook.

'Next Wednesday, I invite you to sit down and listen as
we ask, "Who was Casey Williams?" Thanks for joining me.
Ciao.'

I press the button for the next track and sit back in my chair.
I wave at Josie Manners through the glass window as she slides
into her seat for the six to eight time slot.

'That was massive,' Charlie says, putting her arm around me. 'You nailed it.'

'Thanks.' I look over at Sarah, who is watching the text line.

She looks up. 'You should read this stuff. Josie's following it up on her show now. You completely floored them with the gender revelation. Some people are getting quite snaky, saying it was a cheap trick.'

'Good.' I start thinking. 'We can make that work for us, too. Challenge some of those preconceptions. We'll write that into next week's episode. I want to be really sensitive with this one. We need to think about Casey's family.'

CHAPTER 3
SEEKING THE TRUTH

I live in a loft-style apartment, close to the CBD. It's basically one massive living space, with exposed rafters and industrial-style lighting. The upstairs is my bedroom. I guess I bought it to make me feel less isolated when I returned to Perth after living in a similar loft back in Melbourne. I had loved Melbourne, and now I can never think about it without Crowded House's 'Four Seasons in One Day' becoming an earworm for hours afterwards.

In Melbourne, journalism is much easier. Because there is so much diversity, incredible stories are a dime a dozen. Bring in a bigger population, a mix of ethnicity and economics, and stories that are stranger than fiction are your daily reads.

Contrast that with Perth – quiet, small, seaside town that

it is, a journalist is left with slim pickings. Some would argue that's Perth's appeal – safety and tranquillity. So, I guess you're wondering why I returned. Why not go to Afghanistan, Kabul, Saudi Arabia, if I needed a diet of drama and action?

I'd been involved with someone I thought was my true soul mate (at the risk of sounding like a love-struck teen), and it had ended so badly it made me question everything about my life. Basically, I fled, back to an environment where I could recalibrate, see my parents, catch up with my friends and then, after licking my wounds long enough, step back into the real world.

***

Sarah and I sit at my coffee table. Every surface is strewn with documents, folders, transcripts and recordings. Our Chinese takeaway sits cooling in its boxes.

'Where do we start?' Sarah says eventually. We've been poring over the papers for hours trying to come up with the structure of the next episode.

'I think we need to start with Casey's childhood.' I sift through the cold noodles with my chopsticks and spear a baby corn.

'We want the listeners to know what it was like growing up in rural Australia,' Sarah says.

'Yes,' I say. I think back to the listeners' comments on the text line on Facebook. 'There's been no support for her so far.'

'Well, I guess it's just that we trotted out the basic details of the case,' Sarah says. 'The response to Jonah wasn't very positive either.'

'So, we want to let the listeners get to know each of them with little interference from us.' I stop chewing, and think. 'But how unbiased can we really be? A topic of this nature is surely going to reflect our own attitudes and values?'

'Agreed,' Sarah says. We sit in contemplative silence a while. When I've reported on cases, I've always gone in with an agenda, always used an issue to defend or support my own world view. There's a certain egotism inherent in that – the assumption that my opinion is the right one. But this time, this opportunity was about presenting two sides to the story. Laying out the case, not based on a personal agenda, but in order to present the truth. And truthfully, I didn't even know what my position was on this case or the people involved.

'How about we try and include everything about the people we're representing?' Sarah says. 'Even if we don't like what that shows?'

'Okay,' I say. 'Then maybe we should start with our interview with Casey's mother.'

CHAPTER 4
WHO WAS CASEY WILLIAMS?

'Hi, I'm Amy Rhinehart and I'm the presenter of *Strange Crime*, a live broadcast and podcast on Radio Western every Wednesday at 5 p.m. Season One is called *Double Lives* and examines the Jonah Scott murder of Casey Williams. In Episode Two, "Who was Casey Williams?", we're going to dig deep into the life of murdered transgender woman Casey Williams. Back in April this year, my assistant Sarah and I tried several times to reach Casey's mother Roberta and organise an interview. However, we had no luck getting through.'

I nod at Sarah – we decided late last night that we would give her some on-air time too. She leans into the mike.

'We take a day trip out to the inland town of Kalgoorlie. By day trip, I mean a six-and-a-half-hour drive along the Great

Eastern Highway, ridiculous, I know.' Sarah has a strong and clear radio voice. I watch Charlie nod in approval. 'It's pretty boring. I hear in August the journey can be quite beautiful, filled with wildflowers, but when we take the trip in April, it's still dry and barren and quite hot.'

'We get our first experience of hostility when we stop for a break and a cold drink at one of the truck stops that line the journey,' I continue. 'Massive rigs are pulled up out front, and inside the relatively cool cafeteria – a cafe would be stretching poetic licence too far – I notice we've immediately gained the attention of two big, bearded men. I assume they're truckers, as evidenced by the vehicles out front, and I don't notice them further until I order our drinks. Picture this: I'm late twenties, I have long blonde hair, which was in a ponytail, and I was wearing a tank top and shorts. Sarah is a few years younger than me, about my height, short cropped black hair – a pixie cut would describe it – and she dresses more in, one would say, goth clothes. That day it was denim shorts, an over-sized black T-shirt and her standard Doc Martens. I hear Mr Men One say, "Look, a couple of lipstick lesbos," and I realise they're talking about us. Mr Men Two's eloquent response was "Nice tits." Already I'm feeling intimidated by the jeering voices and the unbridled judgement coming from two ... can I be perfectly honest here? ... fat, tattooed and ugly men. I try not to make eye contact with them as I sit opposite Sarah in the booth.'

'When you sat down, I said something like "Are they talking about us?"' Sarah says. 'I remember I felt so … really uncomfortable.'

'So we decide to take our drinks as takeaways and head to my RAV4. I hear the words "sweet pussy" and "lesbo lovers" from the Mr Men as we get into my car. I'm aware, as we drive off, of the rainbow pride sticker on the rear window of my car.'

'Yeah,' Sarah says, 'we were in the truck stop for five minutes, and we were still an hour out of Kalgoorlie. I remember wondering what attitudes we'd face when we arrived in the goldmining town.'

'For those of you not from Western Australia, let me give you a brief history of Kalgoorlie. The town was founded in 1893 during the Coolgardie goldmining rush,' I explain. 'It remains reliant on mining – notably gold and nickel – and is also the destination of C.Y. O'Connor's water pipeline, which is still the source for water in the town. For years the town has been plagued with antisocial problems, seething unrest and disquiet. There have been ongoing issues between the Indigenous people and the whites, and it's seen the rise of sex work, alcoholism and domestic abuse. I wonder, as we drive down the main drag of the town, how a transgender kid grows up in a place like this.'

'We follow our GPS to Golden Grove – a suburb formerly known as Adeline, before a major government refurbishment to overhaul the suburb,' Sarah says.

'Right,' I reply. 'A comment on Tripadvisor warns us: "Call it what you want, the neighbourhood is still the same. A scattering of hard-working families and a truckload of troublemakers. Good luck if you manage to never have a problem ... ever". It hardly builds any sense of confidence. The housing is a mix of weatherboard, corrugated iron, and brick and tile. There is a feeling of desperation in the air as we pull up outside the childhood home of Casey Williams.'

'I felt really nervous,' Sarah says. 'I wished we could've organised this earlier. I mean, it kind of felt like we were springing it on her.'

'I felt the same way, too. I knocked on the door, heard a dog – I assumed from the sound of its bark that it was big – and a voice shout, "Comin'!" The door was opened by a small woman. She had long dark hair streaked with grey. She looked at us suspiciously.'

'You introduced us and she said, "Youse those journos that's been ringin' here?"' Sarah says. 'And then you asked if we could have an interview. I was really surprised when she nodded and led us in.'

'After this message from our sponsors, I'll play you the interview we had with Casey's mother.'

I slide my headphones off and look at the clock. Twenty minutes just to create background context. I wonder if I'll make it through all the content in this episode today.

I press play and the interview we recorded, months earlier, fills the studio.

Amy: Thank you for agreeing to talk to us today, Mrs Williams.

Roberta: Roberta's just fine.

Amy: Thank you. As you know, we're doing a radio series on the murder of your daughter Casey and we were hoping to ask you some questions about her.

Roberta: Casey I can tell you nothin' about. But my son, Kenneth Cole, him I can talk about.

Amy: Casey was born a boy on the 15th of September?

Roberta: That's right. He was a boy, I know he was a boy, pushed him out of this very body. The same one I pushed his two older brothers and sister outta.

Amy: Kenneth had older siblings?

Roberta: Yeah, he's what you'd call a surprise baby. I weren't expecting no more kids. His brothers were already up and outta home. Sometimes I blame Janet, his sister, for turning him the way he became. Think she always wanted a sister, encouraging him to dress up and play dolls.

Amy: So, Kenneth demonstrated from an early age an identification with the opposite gender?

Roberta: I don't know what that means. But if it means he weren't doin' what little boys should, then yeah. He never liked playing in the dirt, riding bikes, the sort of thing that my other boys did. Nah, he wanted to wear glittery fairy dresses and grow his hair long. His dad called him his 'Sissy boy'. I always knew he was bound for trouble, that one.

Amy: And did he find trouble?

Roberta: It always found him. Take a look around; this place ain't tolerant of outsiders. And there are plenty of them. You're an outsider if you're white, or an Abo, a prozzie, a homo, a weirdo. This town don't tolerate difference.

Amy: What was Casey's, sorry, I mean Kenneth's, school like?

Roberta: Local government. Has its own problems. Don't know that many normal kids that made it through unscathed. But for someone like Kenny ... [A long pause]

Amy: He was bullied?

Roberta: Oh yeah, constant from the time he was in pre-primary, right until he left and went to Perth.

Amy: Can you give our listeners some idea of what things happened to him?

Roberta: Pre-primary was the start of it. We had a huge fight on his first day, he wanted to wear a pink T-shirt and I said, 'No way.' He started crying, begging me to let him. I warned him what would happen. I said, 'They'll tease you and pick on you.' He pleaded with me, 'Mummy I'm allowed to at home – why can't I at school?'

Amy: You let him wear girls' clothes at home?

Roberta: Yeah. It weren't worth the fight. He was always sneaking Janet's clothes. I figured here at home, who'd it hurt? My husband Tom blamed me for what happened. He said if I hadn't encouraged him, none of this would've happened. He used to say 'He'll grow out of it,' like it was just a phase. But I knew he wouldn't. [Sound of a sniff]

Amy: And so, on the first day?

Roberta: Well, it was really Tom's decision. He shouted at Kenny, told him to put on boys' clothes and man up. Dragged him to the car, took him to the school. But it didn't end there.

33

Amy: What happened?

Roberta: Kenny came home – his face all blotched – he'd cried all day. Said they all kept calling him a boy. I'll never forget it. He asked me, 'Why do they keep calling me a boy, when I'm a girl?'

Amy: And after that?

Roberta: I tried to compromise. I could see that Kenny wouldn't give up. I let him wear girls' clothes when he was at home, if he promised to wear boys' clothes when he was at school.

Amy: Did that make him happy?

[A long pause]

Roberta: Nothing ever made him happy – unless he was dressed like that. Then, the teacher called me up the school. She said she'd told them to line up, two lines, girls and boys, and Kenny wouldn't get out of the girls' line. Just flat out refused. I had to take him home.

Amy: For that?

Roberta: Yeah. The principal said it wasn't about whether he was a boy or a girl but about his disobedience and rudeness. After that, Tom went real hard on him. Wouldn't let him wear girls' clothes at home. Told him he was a boy and to bloody well act like one. And that was the end of that, until he went to my sister's to live.

Amy: How old was he then?

Roberta: 'Bout eight or nine, I guess.

Amy: That must've been hard for you.

Roberta: It was. No one wants their kid to live with someone else. But I guess Kenny liked it there better. He seemed much happier in primary school. But then things just got worse when he went to high school.

Amy: What did the kids at school do?

Roberta: Called him queer. Fag, homo. That stuff. Wrote on his books. Beat him up. He was beat up so bad before his thirteenth, that's when he ran away for the first time.

Amy: But he came back?

Roberta: He didn't want to, but them Child Services brought him back. He'd been living on the streets in Perth city. Don't know what he was doing then. But when he came back that was it. He went full into being a girl – despite bein' bashed all the time.

Amy: What happened next?

Roberta: He went to stay with his sister in the summer holidays. I let him go. I seen how miserable he was. I didn't want him going and being a girl. But I didn't want him stayin' here and dyin' [a muffled sound] but I guess it don't matter no more. He ended up dead anyway.

Amy: I'm sorry if this has caused you pain. [A long pause]

Roberta: Sure it causes pain. What mother wouldn't feel pain? He was my son – I loved him. Now he's dead.

Amy: Thank you for your time, Roberta. We know how painful it is for you to recall the memories.

Roberta: What's the point?

Amy: I beg your pardon?

Roberta: What's the point in going through this? We know who killed Kenny. That scumbag can rot in prison for the rest of his life. I don't see that there's nothin' to gain by this.

Amy: I hope we can understand more from this tragedy.

Roberta: No understandin' is going to bring my Kenny back.

'That was our first introduction into Casey Williams' life when she lived as a boy. By all accounts her life was made pretty hard by a lack of acceptance. Up next, we have some interviews we made while we were still in Kalgoorlie. After the break, you'll hear from Casey's Aunt Minnie and cousin, Raquel.' I look over at Sarah, who is attending to the incoming text line.

'That sounded harder listening to it again,' I say to her. She nods.

'Wow, community opinion is so divided on Mr and Mrs Williams,' she says. 'Some people blame them for what happened to Casey – for being so judgemental.'

'That's ironic,' I say, flicking back to the music track I'm playing.

'Hi, and welcome back. Today we are talking to the family of Casey Williams. What you are going to hear next is an interview with her Aunt Minnie.'

Amy: Sarah and I are leaving Roberta Williams' house. We are both a bit shaken. The sadness and misunderstanding, the life that was depicted, were just so depressing. How do you think that went, Sar?

Sarah: Okay, I guess. I didn't realise how intrusive it was going to feel.

Amy: Yeah, I know, right? When she got so upset I felt like we were really prying into her personal business.

Sarah: I guess it doesn't get more personal than this. How do you think Aunt Minnie's going to be?

Amy: Well, she was the one that responded to your calls, right? So hopefully we can get a different perspective.

Sarah and I are pulling into another suburb of Kalgoorlie. This area looks a bit more maintained, a bit more suburban than where the Williams live. I guess this is it, Sar?

Sarah: Yes, looks like they're waiting for us.

[Engine stops, footsteps]

Minnie: Hi, welcome. This is my daughter Raquel. Come in.

Amy: Thanks for giving us the time. We're just trying to build a picture of Casey's – sorry, Kenneth's – life, growing up.

Minnie: We call her Casey, it was what she wanted.

Raquel: It's been so hard, her gone. I miss her all the time. [Indistinct noise]

Amy: You were close?

Minnie: I raised her like she was my own. She found it hard at home; they just couldn't accept who she was. I don't know if it was different for me because I'm her aunt, but I could see how happy she was when she was left to be herself.

Amy: It must be very difficult for you all.

Raquel: Casey was the warmest, most beautiful girl. Everyone loved her. She was kind and gentle, not a bad bone in her body.

Minnie: When she came to stay with us and we let her be herself, she changed totally. She became that happy, gentle kid again. It was like she didn't have to hide anymore.

Raquel: But the kids at school couldn't handle it. They used to beat her badly. She was always coming home like she'd been in the ring with Mike Tyson. Then she told Mum she wanted to go to Janet in the city.

Minnie: And I let her. I told my sister that if we didn't, I knew she'd do something.

Amy: Like what?

Minnie: I knew she'd been cutting herself. I was worried she might go further and actually kill herself. I thought she'd be better off away from here.

Amy: And for a long time she was?

Raquel: Straight away. When Casey moved to Perth, we were always in contact, on Facebook. She was the selfie queen – always putting up pictures of her beautiful self. She was modelling, then.

Amy: Who did she model for?

Raquel: I'm not sure. But she was earning good money down in Perth. That's how she paid for her boob job.

Amy: Did anyone know where she was working?

Minnie: No, I think it was online shoots and that sort of thing. It didn't matter to us, she looked so happy, all the time.

Raquel: That's how I knew something was wrong. I hadn't seen a post from her for a couple of weeks. I messaged her and texted her: 'Hey cuz, where you at?' That sort of thing. I got no reply. I told Mum.

Minnie: I kept calling her mobile – straight to voicemail. We went back through her Facebook account and realised she hadn't posted anything for over three months. That's when we got scared.

Amy: What did you do next?

Minnie: We filed a Missing Persons report.

Raquel: I didn't want Mum to give them Casey's current picture. I was scared of how it would be seen. How people might judge her – like she deserved what she got or something. But who deserves that?

Minnie: I told Raquel a picture of Casey, as a boy, wouldn't help us find her and it turns out I was right. It was only after the autopsy, when the cops scanned for a boy matching her description, that we got the phone call.

Raquel: It was so awful. [Sound of crying] So awful.

Minnie: The detective called us for DNA samples. They wanted a match against a body they'd found. I had to force my sister Roberta to give hers. I think she was in denial.

Raquel: Then we got the call to go into the police station.

Minnie: And that's when they told us the DNA matched an unidentified person. And that it was her.

Amy: I'm so sorry for your pain.

Minnie: Yes, it's so hard to understand why someone would do that.

Amy: Did you know of Jonah?

Raquel: Casey was always boasting about some hot boy she was seeing. And then she started to mention one in particular who she was super keen on. I guess it must have been him.

Amy: How long was she seeing him?

Raquel: I'm not sure, exactly, I guess it would've been a few months. But what I do know is that Casey was spending a lot of time down at that LGBTQI community hub, in the city. After she left Janet's she had no fixed address, she was couch-surfing; that's what made it so hard to keep track of her. I'm pretty sure someone down there would know more about her city life.

***

After the second episode of *Double Lives* airs, we find ourselves in the midst of a media storm – both online and through the mainstream media. *Double Lives* has cracked through all ratings – we are sitting at number one, for the first time in the station's history. Our podcast is being downloaded at a phenomenal rate and Facebook group pages are springing up, questioning the motive of Jonah, the secret life of Casey, conversations about transgender people and the LGBTQI community and even our place in using real life – crime and death – to make ratings.

I have to admit – that one made me question my integrity, and it crept into my mind that I was doing this to understand something within myself, too. But this wasn't cheap theatre; the further into the story I went, the more convinced I was that there were things about this case that had never seen the light of day.

Charlie gives me another assistant, an intern named Will, whose primary job is looking at the leads and comments we are being sent, working out fact from fiction and monitoring our social media. I'm not sure why, but I have a gut feeling that somewhere in this interactive world of everyone being a producer of media we are going to find something that cracks this case wide open.

I'm listening to the audio files we've gathered from the people we've already interviewed. I play the clip Raquel gave me; it's Casey's actual voice. I pause and play it again. It feels important to use it, but where? When do I give her a voice in this? By the time Sarah arrives at my place, I'm listening back on Jonah's first interview with us.

'Hey.' She holds up a bottle of wine. 'Time for a drop?'

I nod. Our nights are long, and generally alcohol-free, but tonight I just really want a drink.

'Listen to this,' I say, as Sarah places the glass of wine in front of me and curls into a ball among the documents. My loft, these days, resembles the headquarters of a *Criminal Minds* investigation – we've even taking to writing on my full plate-glass windows any anomaly or reference point we want to come back to at a later date. In the setting sun, the words create weird swirls of shadows on my walls. I unplug my headphones and turn up the volume on my Mac. Jonah's voice comes out clear and strong.

'I think I loved Casey. Really loved her. When I met her it was this instant attraction.'

'Where did you meet her?' I ask.

'It was a friend's place … I can't remember exactly who. I'd gone there to smoke weed, there were a few people and then I see this beautiful girl. She has a smile that lights up a room …' Jonah falters. *'I mean, had.'*

'So –' My voice sounds a bit cajoling, like I'm trying to wheedle confidential information out of him. I blush a bit. *'How do you get to talk to her?'*

'I ask my mate who she is. He says Casey. I get her mobile number off him. I'm sitting opposite her – she's talking, she's so beautiful. I text her: It's okay to come over and sit next to me. *I watch her look up, she's, like, so surprised, she looks around and then I give her a little wave. Oh, it sounds so fucking lame when I say it now. But I indicate that message is from me.'*

'What does she do?' I think I sound a bit breathless.

'She stands up,' Jonah says, *'and, oh God, her legs are so long,*

she's wearing this short denim skirt – but she doesn't look slutty, or like the Whore of Babylon. She looks like an angel. And then she crosses the room and sits next to me.'

'*What happens next?*' I ask.

His voice is low and soft, it sounds like he's remembering a joyous day from childhood – one of those that are indelibly printed into your mind – the first day you go to the zoo and see the animals from picture books and encyclopedias come to life, the soft-serve ice cream that drips down the side of your hand, the stickiness of fairy floss against your teeth, and the dizzying ride on the carousel. The perfect memory. '*She holds my hand and says, "Hi there, handsome."*' Jonah starts crying.

I hit the pause button and look expectantly at Sarah. 'What do you make of that?' I say.

'Sounds like a boy in love. Infatuated. Overwhelmed,' Sarah says, sipping her wine.

'I know, right?' I shake my head. 'I know it's wrong to say this, Sar, but something about this whole thing makes me think he didn't actually do it.'

'Why?' Sarah asks. 'Because he sounds … what? Like a nice boy?

'Like an innocent boy,' I say, 'he sounds like a virgin boy.'

'And you think virgin boys don't kill women?' Sarah says. 'ISIS martyrs, anyone?'

'If not a virgin, then a boy deeply in love,' I say. 'Call me delusional, there's just something about Jonah the brutal murderer I just don't buy.'

***

Sarah and I agree that before we structure our third episode, we need to pay a visit to the LGBTQI centre. Despite our teetering stacks of information regarding this case, it appears that the new information is shedding – as one would expect – a different perspective on it.

The centre is not far from the train station – we've called ahead and know we are meeting a woman named Laverne. Laverne is about six foot two, wearing a large floating kaftan and a turban, and greets us with a wide hug and a breathless 'Darlings'.

'Hi,' I say. 'Thanks for meeting with us.'

'Not a problem,' Laverne says, in her deep, throaty growl. 'It's always better out than in.' And despite the non-sequitur nature of the comment, I get it. Being out is, of course, always better than hiding within. We are not being met with any opposition from this community, or from supporters of this community, because they want their voices heard, they want to tell their stories. It makes me consider how the other side, the side of denial and judgement, is so reticent with its conversations.

'You knew Casey,' I say, as we sit on one of the couches.

'*Knew* Casey ...' Laverne slaps her chest theatrically. 'I *loved* Casey. She was a right girl, that one. Would take no shit from no one. Oh, I remember like it was yesterday, when she came barrelling in here, her hair awry – and that was cause for notice in itself, that girl was always pristine, impeccable. "Laverne," she shouted at me, "Laverne, I just got arrested." Now, I'm thinking, oh, Casey, what have you done? But she goes straight on, "I'm on the bus, this big thug is standing over this small girl, harassing and intimidating, and I tell him to back off. He makes some comment about lady boys, fucken lady boys, Laverne, can you believe that? And makes to push me. So, I pepper spray him. The bus stops and I'm arrested for causing a disturbance and carrying a controlled weapon. Me! Not him."

'"Casey," I say, "sometimes you need to mind your business." Well, didn't that get her wound up! "And if we all mind our business, Laverne, who's going to stop injustice in this world?" She was a right one, that girl.' Laverne wipes a tear of laughter from her eye.

'Why did Casey carry pepper spray?' I ask. 'Was she feeling threatened by someone?' I'm wondering if Jonah had already started showing a different side of himself to her. But Laverne's look makes me shrivel in shame and ignorance.

'Everyone is a threat, honey,' Laverne says gently. 'In the world we walk in, you just can't trust anyone.'

47

'Who knew Casey?' I ask, looking around.

'Everyone knew her,' Laverne says, 'but if you're looking for someone who knew her well, I'll introduce you to Jimmy. He's out the back. Hang on.' I watch Laverne bustle to the back door. Her movements are graceful; she seems to shift air as she walks, swirling it with her hand.

There are posters on the wall. I look at them with interest. Crisis lines, group chat meetings, most of them seem to offer some type of support or counselling.

Laverne reappears with a short man – although I get the feeling that next to her, most people would look short. He has the triangular torso of a body builder, wide across the shoulders, and through his thin T-shirt I see the hardness of his pecs. He wears a close-cut beard and has light blue eyes that seem to gleam in his face.

'Hey.' He drops down casually on the couch next to me, legs splayed. 'I'm Jimmy.'

'Hi.' I shake his hand. His grip is firm, forceful. 'I'm Amy, this is Sarah, from Radio Western.'

'Yeah, Laverne said.' He looks at me with those amazing eyes. 'You want to talk about Casey?'

'I'm gathering background information. I just wanted to get a feel for who she was before …' I falter, 'her murder.'

'Yeah.' He looks around. 'Look, I knew Casey well, really well, if you know what I mean.' It seems as if his initial appearance was one of bravado; suddenly his voice breaks. 'We were seeing each other for a while. When she first came here. You know, everyone feels a little lost when they begin their transition. You need to be with people who understand ... I came out about four years ago,' he offers.

'Wow,' I say, and immediately regret it. I feel so clumsy. 'I'd never have known.'

'Thanks,' Jimmy says awkwardly. I shift uncomfortably; he looks a bit exasperated by my remark. My brain is racing. Have I offended him? I meant it as a compliment, but *why* should that be a compliment? I'm so embarrassed by my insensitivity. Then he smiles at me and puts his hands behind his head, his biceps bulge. 'It's still a bit of a thrill when I realise that I'm actually being seen for who I really am. You can relax.'

I didn't realise how uptight I was. The last thing I want to do is come across as judgemental or patronising – but it feels like my every response is one or the other.

'I still remember the first time a shop assistant called me sir,' Jimmy says. 'It made my day, it was like, finally, people see the real me. It's such a relief. So, I *got* Casey. I knew what she was going through. I supported her transition.'

'Was she ...' I search for words, 'modelling then?'

'Yes.' He nods. 'Look, it's a tough gig, trying to get money, particularly to fund any surgery you might want. Sometimes a girl's got to do what a girl's got to do,' he says, his mouth twitching slightly. I feel like there are some deep emotions here, but I sense this topic may be off-limits. I look to Sarah for support.

'Did you know Jonah?' Sarah asks. Jimmy turns his gaze on her and his eyes light up. Sarah's a pretty girl, with her pixie haircut and relaxed goth attitude.

'No,' Jimmy says, 'Casey and I had broken up – if you could even say we were dating. We had a thing, but I knew it was never going to go anywhere. I'd heard her talking to others about some guy she'd met – but she didn't talk to me about him. I guess she didn't want to hurt my feelings.'

'Can I ask why you broke up?' Sarah says.

'Sure. I guess it's complicated. She was still trying to figure out who she was. She had her boobs, she was so beautiful. I think she wanted to see if a "real" man could love her.' There's an edge of bitterness in his voice.

'So, that's when she started dating Jonah?' I ask.

'I guess,' he says. 'I don't know for sure how long it was, maybe a few months, longer perhaps. I'll tell you who would know – you need to ask Nellie. Casey stayed at her house a lot.' We watch Jimmy walk over to Laverne, his gait, movements, everything so masculine.

I wonder what that must have been like, to be that boy trapped inside a girl's body. I can't even comprehend it. He comes back with a piece of folded paper. 'This is Nellie's mobile, she's probably got all the girl talk.'

'Thanks, Jimmy.' We rise and I shake his hand. As we leave, he calls out. 'If you need anything else, give me a hoy.' He smiles and waves. 'Or if you'd just like a coffee even.' He winks, but it's not at me, it's at Sarah.

***

Nellie's mobile goes straight to voicemail. I leave a message, asking her to contact me when she's available. Sarah and I walk down the street. It's dark and the pubs are full, there's a smell of beer and the sound of loud music. Going home to develop the episode is the last thing I feel like doing. My head is full of thoughts jostling for space – I need some down time. 'Shall we go in there?' I nod to a relatively sedate pub; as if I've read her mind, Sarah agrees instantly.

'For sure.' She leads the way in and we stand at the bar ordering drinks. I look around, noticing all the different people. Who they are, what they believe in, how they love, is not revealed by their physical appearance. Memories rise within me and taunt me with their cruel clarity. Involuntarily, I shake my head to dismiss them.

'What did you think of the modelling?' Sarah asks me, bringing me back to the present.

'I don't know,' I say, 'it sounds like there's a lot more to it.'

'Nice euphemism?' Sarah suggests.

'I guess.' I shrug. 'I actually don't want to go there.' Sarah tips her head.

'Because you think it will portray Casey in a bad light?' she says.

'Yes.' I am certain of it. 'How would it look if we went on air and proved she was a sex worker? Not only a victim in death – but then portraying her as possibly a victim in life, too – or worse, exposing her to victimisation after her death. The text line has shown that people are polarised on views such as sexuality and gender. The religious zealots barking about God's plans and Him never making mistakes – aberrations and the like. To put that out there would be to destroy the majority of support Casey has.'

'I thought we said that no matter what we uncovered, we would go with it?' Sarah says. And I know it's not that she wants to demonise Casey; working so closely together over the last few months has made me see how committed to the truth she is – that's what's making her question me.

'I'm not saying we won't go with it,' I say, although I secretly believe I am. 'I'm just saying we sit on it a while.'

Sarah nods, I think this appeases her. 'What did you think about Jimmy?' I ask.

'He's hot,' Sarah says. 'Great body.'

'I think he liked you,' I say.

'Yeah, I got that vibe off him too.'

'Would you?' I ask.

'What?' She laughs. 'Have coffee with him?'

'Yeah,' I say.

'I don't know.' Sarah shakes her head. 'Look, I know who I am – a hetero – I like men.'

'But he is a man,' I argue, although I know exactly what Sarah is thinking.

'Yes,' Sarah replies. 'I don't want to come across as some ignorant close-minded bigot, but I don't know if I could have sex with someone like him.'

'A man without a penis?' I say. 'You don't know what he's got down there – apparently the surgery is quite amazing.'

'I know, I've read about it.' Sarah pauses, clearly unable to articulate. 'It's just that – I don't know, I don't do vagina.'

'But ...' I'm not trying to convince Sarah to go out with Jimmy. I'm really only voicing my own thoughts, testing my opinion, challenging the past and trying to formulate my own attitude. 'Look at that guy over there.' I point to this incredibly hot guy leaning casually against the bar, full of confidence that everyone looking at him sees how hot he is. 'Imagine you were going out with him and then you got to the bedroom and he couldn't perform? Or had a tiny wiener. Or, say, he'd had an accident and lost it somehow – that must happen.'

53

'It did to Wayne Bobbit.' Sarah smiles. 'Chopped straight off.'

'But say you'd been seeing each other and you really loved him and then something happened.' I persist with the idea. 'Would that be the end of the relationship?'

'It would certainly make things hard,' Sarah says, deadpan, 'if you'll pardon the pun.'

I laugh at her joke.

'Of course,' Sarah says, 'suppose you're with someone and then they tell you they want to transition, what do you do then?'

I consider this carefully. There is a part of me that wants to tell Sarah the secret lurking in my past, but I just can't formulate the words.

'I guess that's where it comes down to loving the person – irrespective of whatever they've got in their pants,' I suggest. 'Does love conquer all?'

'And when does a transgender person tell the person they're seeing that they've transitioned?' Sarah says. 'We know that Casey got her timing wrong.'

'And when is the right time?' I ask. 'Could this issue be any more complicated?'

'I know, it's doing my head in ... No more shop – let's drink.'

***

Casey's sister Janet runs a popular hair salon in the middle of the city. Sarah and I stand outside the door and watch Janet fixing the last curls into place on the head of a heavily made-up girl.

'School ball,' Sarah says. I look at the girl. She's pretty and bursting with self-confidence. She's transfixed by her own mature and sophisticated appearance in the mirror. I watch her watch herself. She focuses on the way her own lips shape the words coming out of her deep-red glistening mouth. She watches her hand gestures and the way she flutters her own heavily winged eyes. I see her correct a gesture, and try it again, while Janet is spraying the entire contents of a can of hairspray on the girl's head.

I remember that day. My own school ball. I remember that feeling. Shedding the dowdy and drab school uniform for the strapless lemon lace fishtail gown; the long plait halfway down my back replaced with a curled up-do; the brown scuffed lace-up shoes traded for teeteringly high and painful glittering sandals (which would end up causing numbness in my toes and an ache in my calves for over a week). I remember feeling so grown up, so beautiful. I remember feeling transformed. And later, at the function centre, observing that transformation in my girlfriends. We felt like celebrities, A-listers. Even the boys had transitioned into the next stage of our lives. Adulthood.

I watch the young girl emerge from the salon. She is tentative as the breeze picks at the soft curls that escaped the spray. She delicately picks a recalcitrant hair from the corner of her mouth, and with red-lacquered nails dabs gently at the corner of her eye. She gives me a small smile as she passes.

'You look beautiful,' I say.

'Thank you.' Her teeth flash white against her red lips and she hurries to a waiting car.

Janet is sweeping up the last of the hair on the floor and sees us wavering in the doorway. 'Come in.' She gestures. 'That was my last client. I'll put the kettle on.'

***

As Amy and I sit in the salon chairs, Janet starts talking. The resemblance between her and the photos we've seen of Casey is striking.

'She didn't know what to do.' Janet sips her coffee. 'She showed up at my place in the middle of a torrential downpour. Banging on my door, terrified. I couldn't believe it when I saw her there.'

'She hadn't called?' I ask.

'No,' Janet says. 'She just appeared and she was crying and verging on hysterical. I really thought something terrible had happened. "Hey, kiddo," I said. I just held her in a tight hug. "You okay?"

'She said, "I had to get out of there, you know? I felt like I was being slowly murdered." I remember saying, "Let me dry that mop of yours," and, as is the way of the hairdressing chair – it's better than a confessional – she just started talking. About everything.'

'What did she say?' Sarah asks.

'She told me about the bullying. About Mum and Dad.' Janet rolls her eyes. 'I don't blame them – it's just who they are. They couldn't really see what they were doing to her with their denial. Well, I think Mum might've been more cluey. But Dad – he's just your typical redneck, homophobic racist. Anyway, she told me if she stayed there, she'd die. If not at the hands of someone else, then at her own.'

'That must've been awful to hear,' I say. Janet wipes at her eyes.

'It's the most scariest thing a person can say. I asked her, "Are you suicidal?" And she said, "Yes, I don't want to live anymore".'

'What did you do?' I ask.

'I finished her hair and then I put make-up on her,' Janet sniffs. 'And she was beautiful. Truly stunning. Please don't think I'm up myself, I've never had a problem attracting a boyfriend, but there was something so different about Casey.'

I nod my head. I'd seen it too, in the photos of Casey. She had that undefinable thing that sets beautiful people apart from others. It wasn't that her face was perfectly symmetrical – although this was apparently the one thing that made a beautiful face, as pointed out with such authority by the fashion magazines. It wasn't even that her teeth were perfectly straight … I'd noted where her left eye-tooth crossed slightly over the front one. But they were white – the kind of white that is only possible with the application of bleach and infra-red light, surely. It wasn't as if her eyes were perfectly spaced and proportionate to her face – in fact, Casey's eyes were a little too far apart. But the colour – the blue iris with the yellow flecks – resulted in an unusual green that I'd never seen on another person. There was not one particular identifiable thing, I concluded. It was the combination. A perfect mix from Casey's family gene pool.

'And then, I lent her one of my dresses and some shoes and we went out,' Janet says.

'How was it?' I ask.

'Fantastic.' Janet has more tears in her eyes. 'It was the best night ever. Casey was on fire. Finally free to be herself. She turned heads. She attracted nearly every person in the room. I could see that she finally felt at peace with herself.'

'So, why did she leave?' Sarah asks gently.

Janet shrugs, she looks embarrassed.

'My boyfriend,' Janet says slowly. 'Peter was a bit of a dickhead as it turns out.'

'What did he do?' I ask.

'He made fun of her,' Janet says. 'I'm not sure if it was because he was attracted to her or if he was just a total arsehole. But he couldn't cope with her being around. In fact, I couldn't cope with him, when she was around. He was always calling her "Tranny", not Casey. He'd come out of the toilet and say, "Hey Tranny, you left the seat up," that sort of thing. I should've kicked him out.'

'But Casey left instead?' I ask.

'Yeah,' Janet says. 'She thanked me for helping her. She told me that if I hadn't helped her, she wouldn't have got this far. She said she needed to do it on her own. But I shouldn't have let her.'

'Why?' I ask. Janet is quite upset.

'Because I knew the truth. I knew she wasn't doing this for her, I knew she was doing it for me. She didn't want to put me in a position where I'd have to choose between Peter and her. So she left, to save me. That's who she was. That's what she was like. And I regret it, you know. I broke up with Peter anyway. Found out he'd been cheating with a friend of mine. So, he probably did fancy Casey, and he couldn't cope with what that meant to his masculinity. I wish I'd put her first. I wish I'd saved her – maybe if I'd had as much courage as she did, she wouldn't be dead now.'

***

Sarah and I sit in the car in silence. So much sadness. So many tears. Too many regrets. Feeling the pain of a family whose relative has been murdered is difficult enough. Listening to their memories threw so many more thoughts into the blender that was my brain. Even Jonah, when he spoke of her, had those same sentiments about her appearance, her kindness and her heart.

I shake my head, trying to correlate, yet again, those feelings with his actions. I don't get it. I just don't understand how someone could feel like that and then do what he did to her.

Casey Williams, just when she is finally set free, is murdered.

CHAPTER 5
THE CASE

'Hi, I'm Amy Rhinehart and I'm the presenter of *Strange Crime*, a live broadcast and podcast on Radio Western every Wednesday at 5 p.m. Season One is called *Double Lives* and examines the Jonah Scott murder of Casey Williams. In Episode Three, "The Case", we are going to pull apart the details of the manhunt that led to the arrest of Jonah Scott. Take a listen to this:

> *Tompkins: My name is Detective Sergeant Tompkins and this is my partner, Senior Constable Wade, can you please state for the record your full name?*
>
> *Jonah: Jonah Ezekiel Scott.*

Tompkins: Thank you, can you please clarify that you've waived the right to have a lawyer present?

[A pause]

Tompkins: I'm afraid you have to make it audible for the record.

Jonah: Sorry. Yes I do.

Tompkins: You understand that you have been charged with the unlawful murder of Casey Cole Williams, formerly known as Kenneth Cole Williams?

Jonah: Yes, I do.

Tompkins: You have agreed to assist in our investigations of this homicide.

Jonah: Yes.

Tompkins: Was the deceased known to you?

Jonah: Yes.

Tompkins: And how long had you known the deceased?

Jonah: About two months.

Tompkins: What was the nature of your relationship with the deceased?

[A long pause. The sound of water being sipped]

Jonah: We were friends.

Tompkins: What was the nature of this friendship?

[A long pause]

Jonah: We used to just hang out together.

Tompkins: Were you intimate with the deceased?

Jonah: No. Not exactly.

Tompkins: Was there any physical contact between you and the deceased prior to his, er, her death?

Jonah: Yes.

Tompkins: What was the nature of this contact?

Jonah: Kissing and ... touching ... she gave me a blow job.

Tompkins: By blow job, you mean Casey Cole Williams performed fellatio on you?

Jonah: Yes.

Tompkins: How many times?

[A long pause]

Jonah: Look, I don't know, once or twice, maybe more.

Tompkins: Less than ten times?

Jonah: Yes, I think.

[The sound of a chair scraping the floor]

Tompkins: Can you please tell us what occurred on the night of 12 October?

Jonah: We were in my car, out the back of the Haven –

Tompkins: Sorry, can you please clarify for the record, what the Haven is?

Jonah: It's my home, it's the place I live at.

Tompkins: You are referring to the property located at 8 Long Mile Road in Nannup?

Jonah: Yes.

Tompkins: Please continue.

Jonah: We were in my car and we were making out, kissing and stuff, and I put my hand down there –

Tompkins: By down there, you are referring to Casey Cole Williams' genitals?

Jonah: Yes.

Tompkins: Please continue.

Jonah: And that's when I felt something that shouldn't be there.

Tompkins: Can you please clarify?

Jonah: She had a dick. Sorry, a penis, and I just freaked out.

Tompkins: What happened?

Jonah: I jumped out the car and dragged her out. She was screaming and crying, trying to explain. But I just snapped. I lost control. I had a pocket knife and I just started stabbing her crazily. Like, everywhere. I couldn't see straight, I didn't even know what I was doing. And she's crying and there's blood everywhere and then she falls to the ground and she's crying, 'I'm dying, I'm dying.'

Tompkins: What happened next?

Jonah: I was in this state of shock – I wasn't even sure what was happening, and then the next minute she's up off the ground and she's running towards the trees.

Tompkins: What did you do?

Jonah: I ran around the back of my car. The boot was open. There was a hammer and I grabbed it and ran after her.

Tompkins: You chased her down.

Jonah: Yes.

Tompkins: And what happened then?

Jonah: I grabbed her and hit her in the head with the hammer until she stopped crying.

Tompkins: What did you do next?

[A long pause]

Jonah: Can we please stop for a minute?

Tompkins: Sure. Let's take a break. Would you like a water or a coke? Interview paused at 10.17 a.m.

'What you just heard was the beginning of the confession Jonah made the day he was arrested by police. What I'd like you to hear next is Detective Tompkins, the investigating and arresting officer. I have him in the studio now. Welcome to the show, Detective,' I say, and nod to the policeman sitting opposite me to put his headphones on. He leans towards his microphone.

'Hi Amy,' he says.

'What we just heard was the confession Jonah made,' I say. 'Can you firstly please tell us how you came to find him?'

'Yes, I have to admit it was a textbook case,' Tompkins says. 'Following the discovery of the body –'

'By the hikers,' I interrupt, to give clarity for my audience.

'Correct. I never trust hikers, bush walkers or joggers, they always seem to know where the body is hidden.' We laugh and I give him a thumbs-up – he'd mentioned that line to me in our preliminary interview and I'd told him it was radio gold.

'We sent in divers to find the object used to weigh the body down.'

'This was the concrete building block?'

'Yes,' Tompkins says. 'It was located nearer the other bank, opposite to where the body had washed up.'

'If I can just clarify for our listeners,' I say, 'Casey's body was found on the northern side of the river, but you say the block was closer to the southern side.'

'That's correct. We estimated it was some ten metres in from the edge, just before where the river deepens. It seemed likely that the perpetrator had carried the body and block into the water from that side of the river.'

'I see,' I say, although I know all of this. 'For our listeners, I'd like to point out that we have uploaded a map of the area and a schematic drawing of the discovery of both Casey's body and the block, on our podcast site, which you will find at Strange Crime Double Lives dot com.'

'We began our investigations on the southern side of the river. The closest property to the river's edge is the Haven, which you heard Jonah mention in his confession.'

'Please give us an understanding of what the Haven is like,' I say.

'It's a property of some several hundred acres, with approximately fifty individual buildings, like log cabins, scattered through it. It's the home of a religious group,' Tompkins replies.

'This religious group is known as the Brethren of the Word,' I explain.

'Correct,' Tompkins replies. 'I began inquiries there. I spoke to the Elder, a Mr Jacob Scott, and asked about the occupants of the building closest to the river's edge.'

'Woah,' I say. I hold up my hand, 'Mr Jacob Scott?'

'Yes.' Tompkins nods. 'Jonah's father.'

'He took you to where Jonah lived?' I ask.

'Correct. Don't get me wrong, I didn't think this would be where the killer lived – that seemed way too obvious. I thought the occupant of that building might have heard or seen something suspicious that would assist with our inquiries. Instead, when we entered the dwelling, Jonah was standing in his living room. I asked if he knew anything about the night in question and that's when he told me he knew exactly what had happened.'

'Oh, wow. What did he say?'

'He said, "I killed Casey."'

'Just like that,' I say.

'Just like that,' Tompkins echoes. 'We arrested him on the spot and took him to the station for questioning. He made his confession and signed it.'

'That seems pretty cut and dried.'

'It was,' Tompkins says. 'I've never known anything like it.'

'Why do you think he just confessed like that?' I ask the first question I don't know the answer to.

'Guilt, shame.' Tompkins shrugs. 'Jonah is a deeply religious person and I don't think he could live with his conscience.'

'A form of redemption?' I offer.

'I guess so,' Tompkins says. 'Look, in my line of work you come across some of the worst people in the world. I've met them all – serial killers, rapists, gang members, people who easily commit such acts and have no remorse. No conscience. But Jonah … well, he was a different type altogether. His story fitted: he'd snapped, gone into a rage, and then couldn't live with the truth.'

'And there's no doubt in your mind that he actually did it?' I ask.

'None whatsoever,' Tompkins says. 'He knew the intimate

details of the crime. He was the one who killed Casey and then disposed of her body.'

'Following his confession, he appeared before a magistrate,' I say. 'What was the nature of this hearing?'

'It's the Criminal Mentions Court,' Tompkins says. 'Typically, the charge sheet is read. The defendant enters a plea and then the trial date is set – usually, in a homicide case, a long way into the future, to allow for discovery of evidence and interviews by the defence and the prosecution.'

'But this didn't happen,' I say.

'No.' Tompkins shakes his head, as if still surprised by it all. 'When Jonah was asked how he pleaded, his response was, "Guilty."'

'Thank you, Detective,' I say. 'For our listeners, we have the transcript from the sentencing court – the words are theirs, but the voices are actors.' I press the audio.

Court clerk: All rise. The court is now in session, the Honourable Justice Taylor presiding.

Judge: Please be seated. Jonah Ezekiel Scott, you have been charged with the offence of murder, deprivation of liberty, perverting the course of justice and improperly dealing with a corpse. How do you plead?

Jonah: Guilty, your Honour.

Judge: Do you understand what a plea of this nature means?

Jonah: Yes, I do, your Honour.

Judge: Could you please explain to me your understanding?

Jonah: I will be found instantly guilty of the crimes I'm being charged with.

Judge: You also understand that this forfeits your right to trial by jury?

Jonah: Yes, your Honour.

Judge: And you understand the sentence imposed for a guilty plea?

Jonah: I do, your Honour

Judge: Can you please explain to me what that understanding is?

Jonah: Life imprisonment.

Judge: You understand that life imprisonment means for the rest of your life, with a non-parole period of at least fifteen, but most likely twenty-three years?

Jonah: Yes, I do.

Judge: And so, this is your plea?

Jonah: Yes.

Judge: Then I have no other course but to sentence you to life imprisonment in a maximum security facility.

'You were just listening to the words of the sentencing judge in the Jonah Scott case. We have Detective Tompkins with us in the studio,' I say. 'Detective, what do you make of this?'

'Like I said before, I've never known anyone to admit their guilt in an initial hearing,' Tompkins says, 'and I've been in the job for a long time. Even the judge – an unflappable woman – was taken by surprise.'

'Why do you suppose he did that?' I ask.

'I don't know.' Tompkins shakes his head. 'I suppose he just wanted it over with. He'd confessed. He seemed resigned to just accept his punishment. It'd be easier on the courts if all criminals were such good sports as Jonah, save hundreds of thousands in costs.' Tompkins laughs.

'Did Jonah receive any benefit from pleading guilty and immediately being sentenced?' I ask.

'Not really. Life is life. Although, I suppose he could have ended up with "never to be released", if it had gone to trial and the judge had deemed it so. As it is, the only benefit I see it giving Jonah is the possibility of early release. Remorse goes a long way at parole hearings.'

'So, could Jonah have done it for that reason?' I ask.

'Possibly,' Tompkins says, 'but he'll still serve a minimum of twenty-three years – it's a long time, given there was always a possibility he could have defended the case.'

'But how?' I ask. 'How do you defend a case where you've already confessed?'

'There's a controversial precedent in cases of this nature. It's called the "transsexual advance defence".' Tompkins sips his water.

'Can you explain to us what that means?' I say.

'It's called colloquially the "trans panic defence". It's developed from the "homosexual advance defence", where men who have snapped because they've received unwanted advances from another man – and then go into a rage, ultimately injuring or killing someone – have had their charges downgraded. This is the same concept.'

'Oh, wow,' I say incredulously, 'you mean there is actually a defence that blames the victim? So, a person can plead that they were driven to murder someone because it was the victim's fault?'

Tompkins nods. 'Like I said, it's controversial, stemming way back to archaic law that basically protected a man's honour. Thankfully, there are movements to have it abolished as a legal defence. But, until then ...' he sighs.

'So you're saying that despite Jonah's confession, a defence lawyer could have presented this to a jury and Jonah might have got off?' I ask.

'Not "got off" – he certainly would have faced prison time – but for the much lesser charge of manslaughter,' Tompkins says.

'Why wouldn't he do that?' I ask.

'Again, this is the strangest case I've ever been involved in. All I can say is, I guess he thought he deserved that punishment.'

'Extraordinary,' I say. 'Well, that takes us to the end of this episode. I'd like to thank you, Detective Tompkins, for your time.'

'It's been my pleasure,' Tompkins replies.

I flick to the ads and lift my headphones off. I smile at Tompkins. 'Thanks so much for agreeing to do that. You were awesome.'

'No problem,' Tompkins says. I walk him through the studio and down to security. I wait as he hands his visitor's pass in.

'I know you think Jonah did it,' I say, as I open the glass door. It's a beautiful day outside. Often, being in the studio for hours, with no windows, is like being in a tin can: you forget that there is a world outside. I let the sun hit my face for a moment. 'But did you ever think he gave it all up too quickly? That maybe someone else might have been involved?' I walk across the carpark with the detective.

'Sure.' Tompkins points his keys at the car, it blips. 'But

I knew Jonah had done it. We had the evidence, the DNA, his story fitted. There was no reason to investigate it further. We had a crime, we had a perp, and the perp put his hand up and went, "It was me."' Tompkins shrugs. 'We've got so many unsolved crimes out there, we don't have the resources to try and chase down other people when we've got a perfectly compliant candidate in front of us.'

'It's just so strange,' I say.

'There is nothing stranger than people.' Tompkins gets in his car. 'Especially those with particular religious leanings. Anyway, good luck with the show.'

'Thanks,' I say, and head back to the studio. I think of Jonah, the boy who grew up on a farm, cooped up inside a tiny two-by-four cell for at least the next twenty-three years. I think of that gentle face, his soft voice, his politeness, his terrible remorse. His tears. And I find myself struggling to correlate that version of him with the one of the cold-blooded killer. To me, *that* doesn't fit. I listen to the breeze stirring the leaves on the ground and I know where we have to go with the next episode.

To the Haven.

CHAPTER 6
THE HAVEN

Sarah is driving and I'm scrolling through Wikipedia. The trees pass in a blur. We're making good time because Sarah's foot is clearly made from lead. I glance up to see us pass a sign welcoming us to Margaret River. 'How much further?' I ask.

Sarah keeps her eyes fixed on the road. ''Bout an hour, I figure,' she says. 'Shit. Cops.' Her foot hits the brake hard and I feel myself lurch forward. It's a massive booze bus. We get waved straight through. 'That was lucky,' Sarah says, taking off at a more sedate pace.

'Lucky it wasn't a speed trap,' I say.

'Yeah.' She nods. 'I'm on double or nothing, can't afford to get pinged.' From the way she drives, this news is not surprising.

'Listen to this,' I say, reading from the web page. 'The

Brethren of the Word was founded in 1967 by Reverend Thomas Scott. It was created as a community for disciples to live, learn and worship.' I skim the article. 'Blah blah blah ... hang on, this is interesting. The Brethren is listed as a religious cult and has had several encounters with the police.'

'Oh, yeah?' Sarah looks over at me. 'Like what?'

'Months before the discovery of Casey's body; something to do with a missing woman.' I read it quickly. 'The disappearance of Mercedes Coulter, a British backpacker, was linked with the religious group the Brethren. Mercedes had last been seen cherry-picking at the Haven. Her family hadn't heard from her for a month when they lodged a Missing Persons report. Jacob Scott, the Brethren's Elder, said that after staying for several weeks she had left the farm, hitch-hiking to South Australia. No suspicious circumstances were noted. Mercedes has never been seen again. The Missing Persons report remains open.'

Sarah shivers. 'Did they look in the river? Maybe our boy has more than one victim under his belt?'

'Maybe it's not our boy,' I say, somewhat defensively.

Sarah laughs. 'You're determined to prove his innocence, aren't you? Despite his self-confessed guilt.'

'I know, I know.' I throw my hands in the air. 'I'm the only person on the planet who believes he didn't do it. And I can't even explain why.'

'So, Reverend Scott, hey?' comments Sarah.

'I know, right? This is a family tradition.'

'Can't wait to meet them all,' Sarah says.

***

We pull off the main drag and follow the limestone road named Long Mile. The dust billows up around us; Sarah, as if forgetting the fright she got from the men in blue, is rattling down the track at a high speed. Water from my bottle spills into my lap as Sarah hits a pothole. The car slews sideways.

'Shit,' Sarah says. We get out of the car. The front left tyre is flat.

'Fuck,' I say. I look around. There is nothing to see for miles, except more trees. Our GPS shows us that we are about five miles from the Haven. Our phones have no reception.

'Know how to change a tyre?' Sarah asks.

I shake my head. 'Not really, but men do it all the time. Can't be that hard.'

However, it is. I've managed to fit the jack under the car; it looks a bit wonky and the ground underneath is soft. I try to undo the nuts.

'You've got to be kidding me,' I grunt, as I try to put all my body weight into it. The nut doesn't move. 'These must've been put on with some sort of pneumatic drill.' I'm sweating and breathing hard. Sarah has a go, but the nut won't move an inch.

'There's another four of them, too,' she says in dismay.

At this point we are sitting in the dirt, exhausted. There's less than half a bottle of water and suddenly our situation is looking a bit frightening.

'We could walk.' I point down the track. 'We know the Haven is down there.'

'I guess,' Sarah says. We lock the car and are about to set off, when we hear an engine in the distance. I squint. A white ute comes rattling down the track, and eventually pulls up next to us.

'Looks like ya might be in trouble.' He wears a farmer's hat and is dressed in a blue check shirt. 'Can I give youse a hand?'

'Yes, please,' we say in unison. He grins and gets out of the car, clucking at the jack's position.

'Might just change that first,' he says. 'Don't want the car falling on me.' And we watch in amazement as he swiftly has the car up, wheel off and spare fixed in place. 'That should do it. Name's Rory.'

'Thanks, Rory.' I couldn't feel more like an inept city girl if I tried.

'Whatcha doin' out here? There's nothing down here 'cept for the Haven, and my farm further on.'

'We're going to the Haven,' I say. Rory's demeanour suddenly shifts. His pleasant smile replaced with a tight mouth.

'You some of them religious nuts?' He dusts his hands, as if at the idea of it.

'No,' I add hastily, 'we're journalists going to do an interview.'

'Watch yourself out there,' he says, and his tone is full of warning.

'What do you know about them?' I ask.

'What I know is they've been here since the beginning of time and there's never anything but trouble about them.' Rory drinks from his water bottle. 'Always some shit going down with that lot. You've heard of that crazy American group, the Westboro somethings?'

I nod. 'The Westboro Baptists,' I offer.

'Yeah, well, think of them and then turn up the dial. This lot's much worse. Anyway, take care. Make sure you leave before it gets dark – I've heard some crazy shit coming out of that place.' Rory takes off, and Sarah and I sit in the car.

'That's made me nervous,' Sarah says.

'A bit,' I say. She starts the car and I'm worrying about our safety. Our producer knows where we are, and now so does Rory – but what good is that if we end up in the bottom of the river? I'm trying to rationalise my thoughts. I have images of Satanic worship and rituals in my head – but, I reason, wouldn't we have heard about this before? Wikipedia only had the missing backpacker; of course, Jonah; and some links to anti-abortion pickets. Clearly there is more research to be done on this group. I wish I'd done some earlier.

'We're here,' Sarah says, pulling into the long driveway, which is flanked on either side by dense trees. I'm sure it's only Rory's warning, but I find a chill going up my spine.

'Okay,' I say, and try to sound brave. 'Let's go and meet the family.'

***

After about half a kilometre of driveway, we pull into a clearing. The Haven is remote, that's for sure. But it's surprisingly well maintained. It could be a yoga retreat or a beauty spa. There are several small log cabins dotted around – and through the dense trees, I make out the chimneys and A-line roofs of others located further inside the property.

'Okay.' I get out of the car; there are no signs, nothing to indicate a reception area, but that's because this isn't a yoga retreat or a beauty spa – it's a commune. I walk up to the first cabin and knock on the door. There's no response, no sound coming from inside, and that's when I realise how deathly quiet the place is. It has a feeling of emptiness about it. 'No one home,' I say to Sarah. We try the doors of the other four cabins; same response. There's no one.

I groan. It had been my idea not to call ahead. I had wanted the advantage of surprise – and, truthfully, I didn't think we'd get an interview if we asked. I figured we'd just put them on the spot – it had worked before with Roberta. We knew that there was something in the vicinity of a hundred people living here – so where had they all gone? How did a hundred people vanish? We walk further into the commune, and then we hear the faint sounds of music and chanting.

'Through there,' Sarah says. Now I definitely feel like an intruder, and I'm scared of what we are about to see. Those images of Satanic worship won't leave my mind. There's a large building in the middle of a clearing. It looks like a church, and the music and chanting are getting louder. Sarah looks at me and shrugs. I walk up to the front door, which is wide open. Inside is a colourful display of robes – yellow, orange, red, purple; and the people wearing them – men and women, young and old – are moving around the walls of the church in a type of conga line. If it *is*, in fact, a church; there are no seats or pews, just big colourful cushions against the walls. The Brethren are singing and swaying to the playing of the guitarist who's in the front of the line, and there are tambourines being rattled. They're chanting 'Baba Nam Kevalam' over and over, and then I notice – to my horror – that there is an infant child sitting naked in a shallow bronze vessel, covered in flowers. Sarah grabs my arm as we stand in the doorway waiting for what they are going to do. A man dressed in purple robes bends down and picks the child up – he holds it in the air – it's a boy.

'Welcome, Maneesh,' he says, and kisses the boy's forehead. I'm still waiting for him to pull out a knife and slice the child's throat, but everyone is cheering and throwing flowers, hugging and kissing each other. A woman in golden robes takes the child, sits on a cushion and pulls a large and heavy breast out to start feeding the child, who suckles hungrily at it. She glances up and sees me and Sarah at the doorway. I'm embarrassed to be caught staring, and then even more so for intruding. A woman seated next to her rises and makes her way over to us.

'Hi,' she says, smiling. 'Welcome. I'm Patsy.'

'Hi,' I say. 'Look, really sorry for intruding on your ...' I wave my hand.

'Our naming day,' Patsy says. 'It's fine, no drama, all are welcome in the hall of the Brethren.'

'Okay, thanks.' I'm still feeling awkward, and now, a lot like a phoney. 'I'm Amy and this is Sarah.'

Patsy leads us into the middle of the hall and indicates that the three of us should take our place on some of the cushions that have now been scattered through the hall for the congregation to sit on.

'What were you singing?' Sarah asks.

'Oh, Baba Nam Kevalam.' She closes her eyes momentarily, I think she is swaying. 'It's Sanskrit, meaning "only the name of the beloved".'

'Oh, I see, 'Sarah says. 'I thought this was a Christian organisation?'

'It is,' Patsy says. 'But the Brethren embraces other cultures and influences as well as the scripture of the Lord. We believe in meditation, mantras and yoga, to clear the mind for the one true focus on God.' Yoga. I knew it!

'So, how can I help you?' Patsy asks. 'The Haven is a long way off the beaten track. We don't normally have people stumble across us – usually this is a part of their journey. Their destination.' She has the kind of sing-song voice that you really expect someone dressed like her, sitting in a place like this, would have. Do they cultivate it, or is something they start out with?

'We're journalists,' I say – does she flinch? 'And we'd really like to speak to Jacob Scott.' There, it's out. Her calm demeanour is back. She rises.

'Not a problem,' she says. It's no surprise to me that Jacob is, of course, the purple-robed man. He comes over and sits down cross-legged in front of us. I feel like I'm looking into Jonah's eyes.

'Names are so important,' he begins. He has a deep and cultured voice. 'They can be the one true thing that defines who we are, how we walk through this life and into the eternal future. My son Jonah's name is from the biblical story of the whale. Are you familiar with it?'

I nod my head. 'A bit.' I feel like the kid failing Sunday school.

'When God called to Jonah and told him to preach to

Ninevah, Jonah was very angry. The people of Ninevah were one of Israel's greatest enemies and Jonah wanted nothing to do with them.' I notice that some of the congregation are moving closer to us on the floor, listening to Jacob's soft and melodic voice. 'Defiantly, Jonah tried to run from God and headed by boat to Tarshish, so God sent a great storm and the sailors on board the ship decided it was Jonah's fault, so they threw him overboard. As soon as Jonah was in the ocean the storm stopped.

'A big whale, sent by God, swallowed Jonah, to prevent him from drowning. Inside the belly of the whale for three days, Jonah prayed to God, repented and praised God. Then God had the whale throw Jonah up on the shores of Ninevah.' The chatter has stopped and all eyes in the room are on Jacob. Jacob smiles at us.

I'm a bit confused. I'm not sure what to make of this story, or of its message.

'My son Jonah now sits in the belly of the big fish. His three days will be long, but time enough for his repentance and his forgiveness from God,' Jacob says. 'It is Jonah you've come to talk about?'

'Yes,' I say. 'We were really hoping to get a feel for him, his upbringing ... and what could have motivated him to commit such a crime.'

'Come with me,' Jacob says. 'I am more than happy to take

you around and show you what we do here at the Haven. These are my other sons, Cain and Daniel.'

'Not Abel?' Sarah mutters. I try not to giggle; it must be nerves, and this place is still wigging me out a bit.

'No.' Jacob smiles, looking even more like Jonah. 'That would be an awful self-fulfilling prophecy, wouldn't it?'

Cain and Daniel are taller than Jacob, who appears taller than Jonah. They are well-built, and shake our hands with a strong farmer's grip. 'Welcome,' they both say.

Okay, so at this point I'm starting to feel uncomfortable. It's a love fest – everyone is all smiles and generosity, and it feels like one big phoney front for something sinister. I feel like I'm being lured in.

***

We walk through the grounds. Past the grove of trees is farmland. Rows and rows of fruit trees in meticulous straight lines. It looks like an advertisement for canned fruit: young women and men, dressed in denim shorts and checked shirts, pluck apples and oranges from the trees and fill their wicker baskets.

'Most of our workers are backpackers,' Daniel says, leading the way. I think of Mercedes, the missing fruit picker.

'The Haven is an eco-friendly farm,' he continues. 'We believe there is no place for chemicals or pesticides in the production of food. We are one hundred per cent organic.'

'We grow fruit, mostly apricots, apples and berries, which we sell wholesale, as well as our line of jams and marmalades. We have a bakery and a poultry farm – through there,' Cain adds. He is pointing towards several industrial-sized buildings.

'My boys run the farm,' Jacob says, putting an arm around Cain. 'I'm in charge of the spiritual journey.' I must admit the layout is pretty impressive and the philosophy seems solid, so why does my cynical mind keep waiting for the evil stuff to be revealed?

'Jonah was in charge of the fruit production before his arrest. Cain has had to add that to his list of chores.' Jacob smiles fondly at the eldest son.

'We all do what we can,' Cain says. 'If you'll excuse me, Daniel and I need to get changed.' He pulls at his orange robe. 'Back into farmer threads – the eggs aren't going to collect themselves.' We watch them walk off.

'There's no machinery here?' I ask.

'The basics, but most of our production is hands-on. Idle hands are the devil's workshop,' Jacob says. We are now standing in front of a small cabin – it's at the most remote part of the farm and backs onto a more heavily wooded area. 'This was Jonah's home.' Jacob pulls out a set of keys and unlocks the front door.

***

It's neat and tidy, a living area with a kitchen, and a bedroom and bathroom. It looks exactly like a holiday rental villa you'd expect to find anywhere in the state. I look through the kitchen window into the darkness of the forest.

'Through there,' Jacob says, opening the back door, 'is where they discovered Casey.' He leads us down the steps and through a faint trail to the water's edge, some ten or so metres away. If not for the fact that it was a crime scene, it would be beautiful. The river runs gently and there are large birds with curved beaks wading along its edge. 'Ibises,' Jacob says, as one takes off, flapping its huge wings. 'Casey was found over there.' He points to the other side of the riverbank. I recall the vision I've had of her since beginning this journey – that awful white and green swollen corpse. I shudder. Jacob notices.

'Come,' he says. He takes us back past the farm buildings to the cabin that I knocked on initially. Inside it is comfortable and homely.

'Can I offer you a cup of tea?' My mind screams, *don't drink the Kool-Aid*, but I nod anyway. Sarah asks for a glass of water. Jacob invites us to sit at the table.

'It was a great disappointment to discover Jonah's crime,' Jacob says, placing a cup of tea in front of me. I find his choice of word – disappointment – odd. 'He was always the most gentle of my sons. He was the one who would hand-rear the orphaned lamb, nurse the chicken with the broken wing.' Jacob's eyes mist. 'To believe he could do something so vicious …' He falters, and shakes his head. 'But now he is receiving just and fair punishment for it.'

'Did you ever meet Casey?' Sarah asks.

To my surprise, Jacob nods.

'Yes, the day before her murder. Jonah had brought her here to the Haven for a big family ceremony we were having. She seemed like such a lovely girl. I never would have known that she was not actually a girl.' Jacob shakes his head almost angrily. 'I still don't understand that. Why on God's earth someone would deny who they are. Would so arrogantly question God. "No one whose testicles are crushed or whose male organ is cut off shall enter the assembly of the Lord," Deuteronomy 23:1.'

'But Casey's weren't,' I argue. I have to admit, I've been waiting for this.

'To do such a thing is to cut oneself off from the congregation of the Lord,' Jacob says.

'"There is neither Jew nor Greek, there is neither slave nor free, there is no male and female, for you are all one in Christ Jesus," Galatians 3:28,' Sarah says gently. I'm impressed with her scripture, and I see Jacob is too.

'Yes, all Christians are considered the sons of God. But if

any man does not have the Spirit of Christ, then he is none of this.' He leans closer and I see it, finally, that fanatical look in his eyes. '"A woman shall not wear a man's garment, nor shall a man put on a woman's cloak, for whoever does these things is an abomination to the Lord, your God,"' Jacob's voice is still calm and controlled. 'Deuteronomy 22:5.'

'"For there are eunuchs who were born that way from their mother's womb; and there are eunuchs who were made eunuchs by men; and there are *also* eunuchs who made themselves eunuchs for the sake of the kingdom of heaven. He who is able to accept *this*, let him accept *it*," Matthew 19:12,' Sarah retorts calmly.

'Since the Fall, all humans are born suffering spiritual and physical deformities due to sin's ravages,' Jacob says. 'We are all broken in one way or another. Scripture does not condemn or prohibit such brokenness. Rather, scripture prohibits expressing our brokenness in ways that are contrary to God's creative design.' Jacob's voice has lost its calmness and now has the rising tenor of an evangelist. 'Leviticus 18:22: "You shall not lie with a male as with a woman; it is an abomination." Leviticus 20:13: "If a man lies with a male as with a woman, both of them have committed an abomination; they shall surely be put to death; their blood is upon them."' His fist comes down with such force that the water in Sarah's glass jumps. While I'm enjoying Sarah taking it straight up to him,

I see that scripture ping pong could go on for eternity.

'Are you saying that Casey deserved to die?' I ask. Jacob turns his intense gaze on me.

'No,' he says, his voice suddenly soft again. '*I'm* not saying that – it is the Lord who says that.' I see him glance at the clock on the mantelpiece. The sun is setting and we've got a three-and a-half-hour drive ahead of us, if Sarah sticks to the speed limit. I stand and offer my hand.

'Thank you, we've taken up so much of your time,' I say.

'You're more than welcome.' He turns to Sarah. 'I enjoy having such rigorous discussions about scripture, particularly with people who know the works intimately.' I think this is a barb directed at me. 'You are always welcome here to discuss and find your way on your spiritual journey.'

'Thanks,' Sarah says. Jacob stands at the doorway and waves as we drive off.

'I didn't know you could quote scripture,' I say. 'It was pretty impressive.'

'Yeah,' Sarah says, turning onto Long Mile Road. 'For the first twelve years of my life, I was raised as a Mormon.'

'You're kidding me,' I say, but then I realise that I haven't known Sarah long, and that prior to working on *Strange Crime*, I had barely spoken to her.

'Yep,' she laughs. 'I remember the day I came home from school and my parents sat me down for a talk. They told me they'd decided to leave the Mormon faith. I was thrilled. But then they told me they were becoming Jehovah's Witnesses and the thrill turned to agony.'

'No birthdays and Christmases,' I say.

'Exactly. Fancy doing that to a twelve-year-old,' Sarah says. 'I lived all my teenage years on a diet of scripture and sermons. That type of conversation was just how we spoke at home in usual conversation. If you could find scripture to support your argument, you usually won.'

'What did you make of Jacob?' I ask.

'What a creep. Look, I know these overly zealous types – but there was something underneath that façade which seemed ... I don't know, dangerous.'

'Yeah, I got that impression, too,' I say. 'It was like this smiling love-fest hiding something putrid.'

'It's called love bombing,' Sarah says, 'a standard technique to suck you in.' We drive in silence for a while. Sarah's flicked the headlights on and is driving at a legal speed.

'I've got to agree with you,' Sarah says eventually. 'About Jonah.'

'Really?' I'm pretty excited. 'You've seen the light! Amen, sister.'

'Yeah.' Sarah sounds pensive. 'I'm not convinced he didn't do it, but I feel like if he did, he didn't do it alone.'

'The brothers?' I ask.

'Yep,' she says, and then glances over at me, 'and the father, too.'

***

The next day Sarah comes over early, bearing coffee and croissants. 'Thanks,' I say. She's bought me a latte double shot, with no sugar. She knows exactly how I have my coffee, as that was one of her major jobs before being put on this show with me. I realise how badly under-used she was. She is proving to be my right hand. 'Where do we want to go with the depiction of the family?'

'What would be great,' Sarah says, 'would be to find something big that we could use. I think I'll try and find Mercedes' family in the UK. Maybe there's something explosive in that?'

I nod. I like the way Sarah's thinking. I want to depict them as the sinister cult I believe them to be, but we don't have anything substantial. Aside from Jonah's murderous rage, obviously. My mobile rings. Sarah is busy googling. I answer it.

'Hello.' It's a woman's voice. 'Is this Amy Rhinehart?'

'Speaking.'

'My name is Nellie, you left a message for me.'

'Right,' I say. Sarah looks up, interested. 'I was hoping you would be able to talk to me about Casey Williams.'

'Sure,' Nellie says. 'I know everything there is to know about Casey.' I feel a thrill run up my spine. This could be what we've been looking for.

'Can we meet?' I ask.

'No problem,' she says. 'In an hour? Do you know Simply Beans?'

'Sure,' I hang up and look at Sarah. 'Forget Mercedes for now. We've got to meet Nellie. I think we're going to find out a lot of answers.'

***

We're sitting at a table in the back of the cafe, and I know it's Nellie as soon as she pushes open the door. She is tall, her hair is long and black, and she has a full face of make-up, right down to eyelash extensions. She wears tight jeans, a tight T-shirt and teetering stilettos; she has a silk scarf wrapped around her neck. Heads turn as she enters the room – she's quite breathtaking.

'Hello.' She has a deep, throaty voice, like Laverne.

'Hi, I'm Amy and this is Sarah.' I pull out my phone. 'Is it okay to record this?'

'Sure,' she says. 'I've got nothing to hide.'

'What do you want to know?' she asks, after we order coffee.

'Everything you can tell us,' I say. 'How did you meet Casey?'

'At the centre,' Nellie says. 'She was new and needed a friend. Like Jimmy, I know what it's like to be in that state of transition. You just want to help out.'

'She stayed with you?' I ask.

Nellie nods. 'In the beginning. I helped her get some work. She stayed on my couch for the most part.'

'What sort of work?' Sarah asks. I shoot her a warning look.

'Odd jobs,' Nellie says, 'a bit of photography. A couple of dates, that sort of thing.' Sarah opens her mouth to ask something but I jump in – I don't want to explore this, I want the other information that I'm sure Nellie has.

'Where else did she stay?' I ask.

'More recently, she'd stay with Jonah – when he came up to the city with his fresh produce. A hotel room.'

This is big news – I can barely contain my excitement. 'How long had she been seeing him?' I ask.

'I think it was about eight months,' Nellie says. 'Maybe longer; it felt like he'd been hanging around for years.'

I look at Sarah – eight months! Jonah indicated it had been less than two – and in hotel rooms?

'Did you know him?' I ask.

'Yes.' Nellie nods. 'He'd come around and say he was here to take his princess away for some loving time.'

'Loving time,' I repeat.

'Oh, yes,' Nellie nods again. 'They were so loved up, always touching each other and kissing, until I'd say to him, "Go get your hotel room".' She laughs at the memory of it.

'He'd talk about sex?' I ask.

'Yes,' Nellie replies. 'He'd tease me all the time. Casey loved him – I could see it. She was always so happy when he was around, so sad when he had to go back to the farm. She lived for his visits.'

'Just to get this right,' I say, unravelling all the information in my mind. 'Jonah knew Casey was a transgender woman.'

'Of course he did,' Nellie says. 'That was one of the things I loved about Jonah. He once told me, "It's the person I love, Nellie. The girl that she is and that's just another part of her".'

'So what did you think when he murdered her?' I ask.

'I didn't believe it.' Nellie's eyes fill with tears. 'I didn't believe at first that she was dead. My beautiful baby girl. And then I didn't believe it when he said he did it. I didn't know why he'd say it. I didn't know why he'd say she was a liar, that she had deceived him. All I could think was that something went terribly wrong down there on that farm.'

'You know he was part of a religious cult?' I say.

'I warned Casey about that. I said to her to be very careful – but she didn't listen. She thought that her love for Jonah was bigger than everything else, even other people's dangerous beliefs.'

'Did Jonah ever talk about his family?' I ask.

'Sure,' Nellie says. 'He said how he never really fitted in with them. He was the black sheep. He believed in God, he believed God didn't make mistakes and this was how God wanted Casey. He couldn't believe that she was an abomination, I think that's what he said. He said she was God's child and God's message was one of love.'

'Why did they go down to the farm that night?' I ask.

'It was a family bash of some kind. I'm not sure, exactly. But Jonah wanted his family to meet Casey. I think he was so deluded by love for her that he thought they'd accept her, as he did.'

'Do you think they picked her as transgender?' I ask.

'It's the only thing I can think of,' Nellie says. 'Look, there's no definitive answer I can give because both cis and trans women can have masculine and feminine features. But knowing Jonah's acceptance of Casey, I can only conclude that someone at that farm clocked her.'

Nellie talks to us for another hour and then has to rush off quickly.

'Work,' she says, grabbing her handbag. 'Anytime you ladies need to know something, you've got my number.' We thank her and watch the taxi pull up out front and Nellie slide into the back.

'Work, hey?' Sarah says.

I sigh, I don't like the way she automatically assumes the worst, she's like a dog with a bone.

'We need to focus on this,' I say, 'not that.'

Sarah shrugs – she's miffed with me, but ultimately it's my show. What we choose to include is up to me.

'What do you want to look at first?' Sarah says petulantly. I shake my head. Jonah has definitely been lying, but why? What is he covering up? Is it his shame – did he get called out by his family and murder her to try and hide it? Or is he covering up for someone else?

CHAPTER 7

THE MISSING BACKPACKER

Sarah and I work at a frenetic pace, trying to pull the information together that we need for the next episode. I know that our exposure of the Brethren of the Word is going to be massive. Sarah is determined to find something on the missing backpacker Mercedes Coulter. The further into the Missing Persons report she goes, the more convinced she is that Mercedes' disappearance is linked, somehow, to Casey's death.

'Look at this,' Sarah says. 'Her family list her missing in January – by all accounts Casey was already dead.'

I run my eye over Sarah's timeline. Casey's body was discovered some three months or so after her death, in January. If Mercedes was last spoken to by her family in December, then she was definitely on the farm at the time of Casey's death in October. 'Why was her disappearance not seen as suspicious?' I ask Sarah.

'Okay,' Sarah says. 'I spoke to the police officer who took the report – apparently over 300,000 people go missing every year.'

'You're kidding me?' I can't believe the number.

'Yeah, so,' Sarah reads from her notes, 'police spend about fourteen per cent of their time looking for missing people. It's something in the vicinity of a thousand cases a month. They get ranked in risk levels. The cop told me Mercedes' disappearance was a low risk; there was no apparent threat of danger.'

'But after the discovery of Casey?' I say. 'Surely that would have rung some alarm bells? One missing person shows up dead – coincidence, or pattern?'

'That's what I thought, too,' Sarah says. 'But the cop was insistent that because only one per cent of missing people ever show up dead – and it's usually through misadventure or suicide – then it was highly unlikely that Mercedes was also dead.'

I shake my head. 'To me, it sounds more likely.'

'I know, but then he showed me this.' Sarah pulls out a police report. 'There were bank transactions on her account in January – and then later, in February. This one' – Sarah holds the paper up to me – 'was from an ATM in Sydney.'

'Sydney,' I say. 'So, what if it's someone using her card?'

'There's this,' Sarah adds. 'A photograph of the woman at the ATM.'

I look at the picture. It's pretty poor quality and the person is looking down, to avoid the camera. I place it next to the picture we have of Mercedes. Mercedes has long dark hair and a very angular face, with prominent cheekbones. Sure, this could be her – but it could also be any other woman of the same height and build. 'It's not exactly definitive,' I say.

'No,' Sarah agrees. 'But it's enough for the cops not to continue a country-wide manhunt. At this point they're leaving her file open – but they're convinced she's alive and well somewhere.'

'So now what?' I ask. Mercedes looked like such a good lead. In my mind she was going to be the link to the sinister carry-on down at the Haven. A pattern of bizarre rituals and sacrifice. I know I was demonising them in my head, but unless you've looked into the eyes of a fanatic, you probably can't really know how terrifying they are.

'I'm Skyping her parents.' Sarah looks very proud of herself. 'They've agreed to talk to me.'

***

I listen in as Sarah connects to the Coulters in Essex, England. On the monitor, the Coulters look like anyone else's mum and

103

dad. A middle-class couple, in their mid-sixties, nice furnishings behind them, all pretty normal.

'Thanks for agreeing to talk to me,' Sarah says.

'No problem, dear.' Mrs Coulter has a strong clipped British accent. Mr Coulter nods.

'We're doing a show about the murder of Casey Williams, and in our research your daughter's name came up as last being seen at the place Casey was murdered – the Haven,' Sarah says.

'Yes, we know about your show, it's getting a bit of airtime over here, too.' Sarah raises her eyebrows at me. 'Everybody seems to enjoy a good conversation about murder and intrigue, don't they?' Mrs Coulter nods at her husband.

'Can you remember the last time you spoke to Mercedes?' Sarah asks.

'I can't be exact on the date now, but it was roughly around early January, or late December. Oh, my mind doesn't retain things like it used to,' Mrs Coulter says apologetically.

'Right, and did Mercedes give any indication that things weren't right?'

'No, dear, not at all. She was so happy, she loved that farm and the people. We thought that she'd never leave.'

'And then you didn't hear from her?'

'Yes, that's right.' Mrs Coulter shakes her head. 'Mercedes was what you'd call a free spirit. Always drifting around, doing her own thing. When she decided to travel to Australia, we weren't worried, aside from the spiders and the snakes. You've got a few nasty creatures down there, don't you?' Mrs Coulter laughs. 'She had a level head, always acted responsibly. Every couple of weeks she'd update us on her travel plans. That's why we eventually filed the Missing Persons report. Four or five weeks of no contact was just so unusual – it was as if Mercedes had simply vanished.'

'And the police found nothing?' Sarah asks.

'That's right. They questioned the people at the farm, who said Mercedes was hitch-hiking to South Australia. I didn't like the idea of her doing that – especially because we remember that Milat fellow. But the police were convinced there was no sign of any foul play. The policeman, a lovely young chap, said if people don't want to be found, they won't be.'

'And you've never heard from her?'

'No dear, not a word,' Mrs Coulter says.

Sarah continues talking to the parents a while longer, and then signs off. We look at each other.

'That was weird, right?' Sarah says.

I nod. It *was* weird – the parents seemed virtually emotionless. Their daughter has been missing for over two years and there isn't one sign of grief – or tears, even.

'British stiff upper lip?' I say.

'I dunno.' Sarah shrugs. 'It was so robotic, so ... almost scripted. It just didn't feel genuine.'

'Do you think Mrs Coulter is lying?' I ask.

'I'm not sure – but what I am sure of is that something strange is going on.'

CHAPTER 8
THE BRETHREN OF THE WORD

'Hi, I'm Amy Rhinehart and I'm the presenter of *Strange Crime*, a live broadcast and podcast on Radio Western every Wednesday at 5 p.m. Season One is called *Double Lives* and examines the Jonah Scott murder of Casey Williams. In Episode Four, "The Brethren of the Word", we are going to take you on the road trip my assistant Sarah and I took last week to a beautiful corner of the state's south west and see where Jonah grew up. Due to the amount of content in this episode we've had to divide it into two parts. We'll air Part Two next week.

'Before we go there, I'd like you to listen to this interview that I conducted with Frank Moore, a world-renowned investigator into cults. Frank has worked for the FBI, and more recently he has been heading up a special task force that deals with identifying cults and deprogramming participants.'

Amy: Welcome to the show, Frank. It sounds like a very interesting job that you have.

Frank: Thanks for having me. Yes, it is, extremely interesting.

Amy: You've been in this field for over thirty years – can you tell us what marks a group as a cult, instead of, say, a religion?

Frank: I guess it goes back to your initial impression of the so-called cult. Generally, if it walks like a duck, quacks like a duck, then it's probably a duck.

Amy [laughs]: So for any of our viewers not familiar with a cult, what would that walking and quacking look like?

Frank: It seems obvious. It's like looking at, say, pornography versus nude artwork. You know the difference when you see it. When we compare a cult to a religious group, the very first thing we notice is their similarities. It is their subtle – and they can be very subtle – and gradually revealed differences that make them stand out.

Amy: Right. Can you please give us an example?

Frank: Sure. Cults are ultimately about gaining and keeping excessive control. In fact, all cults have very tight rules and restrictions that look like they come from a universal handbook of dos and don'ts. The following few points would be a basic checklist when facing a so-called cult. Firstly, is there a charismatic leader whose personal agenda offers the elixir of life? Their knowledge and understanding can solve personal, moral, spiritual problems within the follower and the world in general. Devoted faith in the leader becomes the primary role of the follower, who in turn acts as the enabler of the leader.

Amy: So, the names of very famous cult leaders spring to mind ... Charles Manson and Jim Jones.

Frank: Jim Jones was a particularly dangerous character. His influence and control were so great, he had over nine hundred people commit suicide in the one night, back in the late seventies. Which leads us to point two: faith in the mission. Individualism is discouraged and ultimately eradicated – the group's achievements are celebrated and memorialised. And the 'mission' might not be something as drastic as 'a revolutionary attack' – which is what Jones told his followers – it could be something seemingly benign, like spreading the religious ideology of the group.

Amy: So, the individual loses their original thinking?

Frank: Exactly. All they can do is parrot the thinking of the leader. So, thirdly, the leader sets up a situation to separate followers from the outside world. Initially this is done through language, but often it's also done through geography, isolation in a remote area. To maintain cohesion and unity in the group, and ultimately complete control, there is a clear division between 'in' and 'out'. Insiders – followers – are told they are 'special', 'chosen', 'accepted'. Outsiders are seen as 'unholy', 'morally corrupt', 'dangerous'. To maintain complete control, contact between the two worlds is discouraged. Contact with family members not in the cult is ultimately severed.

Amy: It's the whole divide and conquer concept?

Frank: That's right; the cult leader must be seen as infallible – possessing all the answers. They are often narcissists with an insatiable need for power, control and, sometimes – as you mentioned with Charles Manson – fame.

Amy: So, at this point, followers are totally brainwashed?

Frank: Generally so. There is another aspect of control operating here and it's through clearly defined reward and punishment, which I would say is the final point. By the

*need to please the leader and ascend to the higher ranks
in the cult, obedient followers are exalted and praised.
Those who don't conform are publicly outed and shamed,
ultimately expelled. Expelled members are never to be spoken
to again. This protects the cult.*

Amy: So how do people get out?

*Frank: It's difficult. They've generally isolated themselves
from the outside world, the fear of not surviving in the
outside world is very real. Most of the time they've seen what
happens to non-conforming followers, so when a cult member
becomes disenchanted, they have to be very cautious. They
are entering a world of danger that threatens to undermine
the stability of the cult.*

Amy: So, what can they do?

*Frank: People I've helped to deprogram always use the
same word when they talk of leaving the cult, and that's
'escape'. When they first present in the cult as 'disobedient',
usually by questioning something, they generally go through
intensive 'confessionals' where they have to outline every
bad thing they've ever done, real or imagined. It's a form of
mental humiliation – designed to make the follower
feel worthless.*

Amy: And therefore, the leader looks more powerful. I'm interested, though, what makes people join a cult?

Frank: I don't think anyone wakes up one morning and thinks 'today I might join a cult'. That's part of the danger of cults – they don't advertise: 'Join us, we'll take away your freedom, your money, we'll turn you into a slave'. They always appear as something else – maybe a self-help group, an alternative-medicine group, even a yoga-meditation group.

Amy: And so that's how people get sucked in?

Frank: Yes. If I went to a new group, I'd ask myself if there is one person there who the others highly revere – someone who presents like the Messiah. If so, chances are you've stumbled on a cult.

Amy: Frank, I asked you to look at the Brethren of the Word and see if, in your opinion, it fits the design of a cult.

Frank: Well, let's put it up against our checklist. Is there a charismatic leader who followers seem to worship?

Amy: Check.

Frank: Is there a mission that all the followers have complete faith in?

Amy: Living according to scripture, does that count as a mission?

Frank: Well, that's interesting in itself – whose interpretation of scripture? Is it just one person's?

Amy: Check.

Frank: Is there a sense of separation from the outside world? Both through language and geography?

Amy: Check.

Frank: And, finally, is there a reward–punishment system? Or a reprogramming system for recalcitrant followers?

Amy: That point, I'm not sure of.

Frank: Well, so far we've met three of the four main criteria – so, I think your duck is definitely walking. We need to hear if it quacks.

Amy [laughs]: Thank you so much for your time here today.

Frank: My pleasure.

After Frank leaves the studio, I look at my monitor. My next audio is cued to go – it's a recording I made when Sarah and I visited the Haven. My voice fills the studio.

'Okay, Sarah and I are en route to the Haven – it's the place where Jonah grew up, the scene of the crime and his arrest. It's quite a drive – but through some beautiful and lush scenery. We've arrived unannounced and find our way to the Hall, where there is a naming ceremony being conducted. The scene is like something you'd expect to see in a film from the sixties about Rajneeshees or Hippies. There is a lot of love and singing in the air.'

The recording of the singing is quite muffled; I had my iPhone in my pocket. *'You get the general idea, right?'* I say. *'We meet the charismatic leader of the group, Jacob Scott, Jonah's father. He shows us around. The Haven is a self-sufficient farm, creating and supplying a range of goods from eggs to fruit, breads and preserves. By all accounts the farm itself turns over about fifteen million dollars a year. Not bad by anyone's standards.*

'The farm relies on its volunteers – group members who live there in cute log cabins, and backpackers from Europe who pass through at seasonal times,' I say. *'Actually, we watched the fruit-pickers and they looked like they were having a good time, right, Sar?'*

'For sure, it looked like a pretty cool place to work,' Sarah says.

'So far, everything seems pretty normal. It's all kinda, oh, you know, just a group of people who care about the environment and healthy living and working together. But then we, or more

importantly, Sarah, get into a religious discussion with the infallible leader Jacob Scott about trans people.'

Jacob's voice, full of authority takes over. *"No one whose testicles are crushed or whose male organ is cut off shall enter the assembly of the Lord," Deuteronomy 23:1.*

"'A woman shall not wear a man's garment, nor shall a man put on a woman's cloak, for whoever does these things is an abomination to the Lord, your God," Deuteronomy 22:5.' The recording has actually picked up the sound of Jacob's fist hitting the table.

'Leviticus 18:22: "You shall not lie with a male as with a woman; it is an abomination."' The rising emotion carries through the airways strongly. *'Leviticus 20:13: "If a man lies with a male as with a woman, both of them have committed an abomination; they shall surely be put to death; their blood is upon them."'* There is a pause in the recording here, and then my question.

'Are you saying that Casey deserved to die?' There is another pause in the recording here too, and then we hear the final words of Jacob.

*'No. **I'm** not saying that – it is the Lord who says that.'*

'So, Sarah, can you explain to our listeners what the atmosphere was like in that room?' I say.

'Sure,' Sarah says. 'Intense. Jacob Scott looked like someone

115

trying to control himself. He sure didn't like being challenged.'

'And his attitude was quite clear about transgender people?' I ask.

'Crystal. His words were, and I quote, "they surely shall be put to death; their blood is upon them".'

'So, now just bear with me here. If you want to apply Frank Moore's "is it a cult?" checklist to what you've learnt about the Brethren of the Word, how many of his points do you think you could check? Let me leave you with a couple of thoughts. If this is the message Jacob Scott tells his followers – that a transgender person "shall be put to death" – then I suggest Casey Williams' life was in grave danger from the minute she set foot on the property. Not just from Jonah, but from the hundred other people who believe in Jacob Scott's ideology. So, then, it doesn't seem a long bow to draw – what if Jonah didn't do it? What if, say, I don't know, it was someone else? A follower, perhaps? Or even someone very close to Jonah?'

In the original script I'd named Jacob at this point, but my producer had been apoplectic.

'Have you even heard of defamation and slander?' Charlie had said.

'It's not that, if it's true,' I said.

'You have no proof!' Charlie had almost shouted. 'In fact, you have the total opposite. A self-confessed murderer! You take his name out.'

'So, thanks for listening to Part One of "The Brethren of the Word". We'll pick it up from here next week.' I look up as Sarah comes barrelling into the studio.

'You're not going to believe it,' she's shouting. 'I've just had a phone call. From Mercedes Coulter!'

***

It doesn't take much to convince Charlie to pay for two airline tickets to Sydney, out of the show's budget. We're getting so much revenue through advertising that I'm actually a bit annoyed with her when she books us economy. But there's no time to argue – we get on the first available flight and touch down in Sydney just over four hours later. At the cheap hotel (another budget-saving deal), Sarah plays me the recording of her phone call again.

'*Hi.*' The voice is muffled like she's trying to disguise it. '*I think you're looking for me.*'

'*Who's speaking?*' Sarah's voice has a hint of excitement to it.

'*Mercedes Coulter,*' the voice whispers. '*My mum contacted me.*'

'*Mercedes,*' Sarah says. '*We'd love to talk to you.*' There's the longest pause.

'*Okay,*' Mercedes says. '*But you have to come to me. And you have to make sure that no one knows.*'

'*Absolutely,*' Sarah says.

'*I'm in Sydney,*' Mercedes whispers. '*Contact me when you arrive. I'll tell you where we can meet.*'

I feel a shiver again. Her voice sounds so … scared. Who is she frightened of? What is she hiding from?

***

We're meeting Mercedes at a small bar, down an alleyway, in the middle of the CBD. It feels like subterfuge. I nervously glance over my shoulder before we enter, to check I'm not being followed. I can tell Sarah is as tense as me. The bar is dimly lit; there are a few patrons sitting in armchairs that have been set up like conversation pits. There is no one on their own. I frown at Sarah.

'I'll get us a drink,' she says. I watch her cross to the bar and I wait, watching the front door. I hear a slight noise behind me, the hairs on my neck prickle.

'Sarah?' the voice whispers. I don't turn my head – Sarah is walking towards me, carrying two glasses of wine, her eyes are wide.

'Amy,' I say. 'Would you like to sit down, Mercedes?' She steps out of the shadows and past my chair. I watch her look around the bar and then slump into the wingback chair across from me.

'Hi,' she says. She looks nothing like her photo. Her hair is cropped short and is blond at the tips. She looks several kilos heavier – her face has lost its angular look and is now round. She wears jeans and a dark T-shirt; it's a generic outfit – this is a person who doesn't want anyone noticing them, ever. 'Sorry for the cloak and dagger.' Her voice retains the same British lilt as her mother's. 'But you need to know that this could put me in serious danger.'

I lean forward and pick up my glass. Sarah has gone back to the bar and returns with a drink for Mercedes.

'Why are you in danger?' I ask.

'Because–' She looks around and then whispers, 'I know things that could have me killed by them.'

'By who?' The hairs on my arm are standing upright. I know exactly what she is about to say next.

'The Brethren,' Mercedes whispers.

CHAPTER 9
THE BRETHREN OF THE WORD, PART TWO

'Hi, I'm Amy Rhinehart and I'm the presenter of *Strange Crime*, a live broadcast and podcast on Radio Western every Wednesday at 5 p.m. Season One is called *Double Lives* and examines the Jonah Scott murder of Casey Williams. Episode Four, "The Brethren of the Word", was divided into two parts. For those listeners just tuning in now, you can download Part One from Strange Crime Double Lives dot com, and I advise it's worth getting the background info before listening to this episode, which I promise you is explosive.

'Since beginning this serial, my assistant Sarah and I have uncovered information relating to this case that has never seen the light of day. We've met with people whose stories were never heard by the police. Why? Because of Jonah's immediate confession and plea of guilty. Had this case ever gone to trial, then it's likely the people we're interviewing would have made the list of witnesses. *To what end?* you might be wondering. *The murderer was already identified.* I know, but stay with me here. From the beginning I've had this gut feeling that Jonah didn't do it – it's driven Sarah and my producer crazy – but now we have people who have witnessed things, telling us stories that are putting major question marks over Jonah's story.

'I'd like to start with an interview we had with a former cult member of the Brethren of the Word. For her safety we have disguised her voice and changed her name. Let's call her Paula.'

Amy: We are meeting in a secluded bar. We've been contacted by a former member of the Brethren of the Word who wishes to remain anonymous.

Paula: I hope you appreciate I have to be very careful here.

Amy: Careful why?

Paula: I can't have them knowing who I am or where I am.

Amy: We have promised to protect your identity. This interview will be edited and approved by you before it goes to air.

Paula: Thank you.

Amy: You seem very scared.

Paula: I'm terrified.

Amy: Can you tell us why?

Paula: You don't know how many of them are out there.

Amy: Out where?

Paula: Here – in the outside world. They could be anyone.

Amy: I've paused the interview, Paula is a bit distressed, her fear is palpable. I realise I'm sitting in front of a person who has been brainwashed into believing the untold power and strength of the Brethren. When she is ready, we continue.

Paula: I escaped after the family ceremony.

Amy: This would be the night that was identified as the evening Casey was killed.

Paula: That's right. I didn't leave straight away – it was a lot later. After I learnt the things that had gone on that night.

Amy: I see. Can you explain to us what this ceremony was?

Paula: It was a wedding. Jacob was marrying his fourth wife. The followers were invited to the ceremony in the Hall. There was a bonfire and barbecue after.

123

Amy: He was marrying for the fourth time?

Paula: Yes – she was to be sister wife four.

Amy: I think I might be confused here. Are you suggesting this was a polygamous marriage?

Paula: Exactly. In the Brethren, once you reach a certain status, you're allowed to take on another wife. I don't think it's considered legal, but it is recognised as a formal spiritual union at the Haven.

Amy: And do many people hold that status?

Paula: It's only men, and so far only Jacob and Cain.

Amy: Did other people leave the cult after this night?

Paula: Yes. After what happened with Casey, I think about three of us – women – escaped.

Amy: Did you talk about it with each other?

Paula: No. Not at all. But we could feel the change in the air. Something terrible was going on.

Amy: Why wouldn't you talk to each other? Weren't you like a family?

Paula: Yes, but we all knew the consequences of speaking negatively about the Brethren.

Amy: What were they?

Paula: You were put through a re-education program.

Amy: I see. What did this entail?

Paula: There was a building, out past the production sheds, referred to as the Clearing House. Anyone voicing any negativity was kept there for days at a time, compiling an audit on their negative thinking. Admitting out loud and then writing down their transgressions against the Word.

Amy: What was the Word?

Paula: It was a manual written by Reverend Scott – it outlined what you were allowed to do and, more importantly, what you weren't.

Amy: Can you recollect any rules in particular?

Paula: Of course. The rule about homosexuality. That it was an abomination in the eyes of the Lord and anyone found guilty would be put to death.

Amy: They actually had that written in there?

Paula: Yes, amongst other things. Everything was supported by scripture.

Amy: You're painting quite a clear picture of control and obedience under the threat of death. I'm sure many of the listeners would be wondering what compelled you to stay?

Paula: I don't know, it didn't start out like that. It was a great community. It was spiritual and loving. But then, I guess, the more obedient you become, the less you question. It had to take something massive for me to open my eyes and see it for what it was. And when I did, I was terrified. I felt the real threat of danger.

Amy: So, what was it that happened that caused your epiphany?

Paula: We all had certain jobs; Jacob called them chores. I was usually a cook in the farmhouse where we prepared meals for the community. After the ceremony, I was sent to the Clearing House. I didn't know who was in there; it's all very secretive, the Brethren don't like the community knowing about who might have transgressed. I see now that it was all part of their control and their presentation of omnipotence. But in order to keep the transgressor focused on clearing the negativity, the processor – the person who conducts the audit – stays out there too. It's a fully self-contained unit. During the reprogramming the transgressor is totally removed from the community, until the processor

*can establish that all negativity has been replaced with
complete obedience and compliance to the Word. My job
was to cook and clean for the pair of them. You are to move
through the cabin with your mind tuned into a different
plane of thinking, not listen to the audit. But it doesn't work.
Well, it didn't for me.*

Amy: Why was that?

*Paula: Jonah was in such a state of distress I couldn't help
but listen.*

Amy: Who was the processor?

Paula: Jacob Scott, and at other times, Cain and Daniel.

Amy: Was that usual? To have more than one processor?

Paula: No – there was nothing usual about it.

Amy: So, what did you hear?

*Paula: Jacob quoted Leviticus 20:13, 'If a man lies with a
male as with a woman, both of them have committed an
abomination; they shall surely be put to death; their blood is
upon them'. And demanded Jonah confess.*

Amy: Did he?

Paula: Not initially. But when Jacob said the blood of Casey was on his hands. Jonah finally confessed.

Amy: I've paused the interview to give Paula a break. She is shaking and seems very agitated. Her paranoia is contagious, and I find myself looking nervously around the bar.

'After the break I'd like to continue with this recording from a cult member who escaped the Brethren.'

I look at Charlie, she's shaking her head at me.

'What?' I say.

'Legal's just gone through the interview – you can't air the rest of it.'

'Why?' I ask.

'It's defamatory,' Charlie says. 'We could get the Brethren breathing down our necks with a law suit if you put the rest of what she says on air.'

'What am I going to run with now?' I say.

'You must have something else.' Charlie points at my computer. 'Or you have to ad-lib for the next ten minutes.'

'Great.' I flick back to the mike. 'Thanks for staying with us. I've just been informed by my producer that what we were about to air is too controversial. While we look further into the allegations made by Paula with our legal team, I'm going to play you something else. This is an interview I conducted with transgender woman Nellie – who knew both Casey and Jonah very well.'

I press the audio and I hear Nellie's voice coming into the studio. I pull my headphones off and quickly type a script so I can conclude this episode. Inwardly, I'm fuming at Charlie.

The rest of the interview had been Paula's – of course I mean Mercedes' – summation of the events of that night. It's true she didn't have any concrete evidence, just what she saw at the ceremony and what she heard at the Clearing House, but it sounds like a plausible scenario. Mercedes basically concludes that somehow Casey was killed by one, or all, of the brothers and Jacob. I so badly want this idea out there, but with no basis in fact I have to keep Mercedes' opinions to myself.

'So, there you have it,' I say lamely. 'Another person who corroborates that Jonah did indeed know Casey was transgender and was involved in an intimate and sexual relationship with her. I guess this looks bad for Jonah. I guess there are plenty of you out there who think this is proof – an actual motive for Jonah's killing. He took Casey to his family ceremony. Somehow, I don't know how, she's identified as transgender, Jonah's confronted about it and admits he has been having sex with her. Then, given the Brethren's radical views on this, Casey must be put to death. Jonah commits the murder. Makes sense. But, you know, I just don't buy it. There is something here that doesn't add up. Keep sending the texts in and join the chat page at Strange Crime Double Lives dot com. What do you think? Was it a motive or not? Did Jonah really do it? Until next week, ciao.'

'Well saved,' Charlie says from the doorway.

'Yeah, thanks,' I say. She can see how annoyed I am.

'Look, Amy,' Charlie says. 'The idea behind this whole show was to go through the strangeness of the case – not to re-investigate, trying to prove his innocence.'

'What if he is innocent?' I demand. 'Stranger things have happened, wrongful convictions and all that. What if the murderer – or murderers – are still out there? What if an innocent man is sitting in prison instead?'

Charlie points at me. 'This is going too far, Amy. Your job is to report the facts, as you find them. I'm putting you on a week's leave.'

'You're doing what?' I shout.

'A week's leave,' Charlie says firmly. 'You need to clear your head. Start thinking professionally instead of so emotionally. Sarah can cover the show.'

'Oh, seriously, Charlie.' I try not to cry. 'This is my show.'

'Yeah, and look at the pressure.' Charlie is more gentle now. 'You've been all over the country; you haven't had any rest. I'm worried about your mental health.'

'Sarah's been with me, too.' I sound petulant.

'I know,' Charlie says. 'But she's not the one up all hours

of the night writing copy and constructing audio. She can do a mid-season recap. We'll call it "The Story So Far". It'll allow listeners to catch up on the podcast – the numbers are going crazy.'

'All right.' Suddenly the idea of having a break looks appealing. I think I am worn out. 'I guess so.'

'It'll be good for you, Amy.' Charlie gives me a hug. 'Get some rest. Chill out. Then you can come back and start to wrap this thing up. I don't want to see you in the studio for a whole week. Okay?'

'Okay, Mum,' I say. Charlie's only ten years older than me, but she is motherly, and I know this concern is genuine.

***

Back home I listen to the rest of Mercedes' interview.

Amy: What did Jonah actually say? Can you recall?

Paula: He said, 'I have committed an abomination: I must be put to death.'

Amy: Did he say anything about Casey? Her whereabouts?

Paula: No. But what happens over the next few days is this constant line of questioning. Daniel and Cain come in at different times. Jonah's never left alone. He's constantly being asked questions and then his responses are told to

131

him. I think it was at this point I could actually see what they were doing, they were brainwashing him – they were making him cover up.

Amy: Can you recall exactly what was said?

Paula: At first it was hard, because Jonah was so upset – crying all the time. At night, I'd hear him from my room. It was terrible. He looked awful – he'd lost so much weight and his skin was a really grey colour.

Amy: It sounds like they were torturing him.

Paula: In a way. So, Jacob would say, 'Did Casey deceive you?' and Jonah would reply 'Casey deceived me.' Then Jacob would provide scripture, it was from Galatians: 'Do not be deceived: God is not mocked, for whatever one sows, that will he also reap. For the one who sows to his own flesh will from the flesh reap corruption, but the one who sows to the Spirit will from the Spirit reap eternal life.' And then Cain would say, 'Those who consider themselves religious and do not keep a tight rein on their tongues deceive themselves, and their religion is worthless.' And this went on and on, day after day.

Amy: It sounds horrific.

Paula: It was. I was exhausted and I wanted to leave the Clearing House. I didn't want to hear any more of the scripture. I realised at that time how fanatical they all sounded. Like zombies chanting. I realised at that point that I was actually scared of them. This was their brother, their son, and they were relentless.

Amy: Did you ever hear anyone say anything about what had actually happened to Casey?

Paula: No. Her death was only ever referred to in biblical terms, like 'her blood'. At the time, of course, I had no idea she'd been killed. I thought this was all about Jonah having sex.

Amy: So, you never actually heard a confession? You never heard any one of them, not even Jonah, admit to killing her and disposing of the body?

Paula: No. This was all about putting Jonah back into line.

Amy: So, eventually they let Jonah return to the community.

Paula: Yes, and that's when I decided to run. I knew I couldn't stay there. I suddenly didn't believe any of it anymore. This wasn't about love and peace, this was about hatred and fear. I escaped that night. On foot.

Amy: On foot – you must have walked a long way.

133

Paula: There was a farm down the road. I went there and begged the farmer to drive me into town.

Amy: Rory?

Paula: Yes, that was his name. He took me the whole way – three-and-a-half hours – I was happy to have been dropped at a train station. But he told me to get on a plane and leave. I did as he said. I came here to Sydney, I tried to disappear. When I heard about the discovery of Casey's body, I panicked. I asked my parents to report me missing. I figured that the Brethren would never go looking for me if it looked like I had just vanished and no one knew my whereabouts.

Amy: You say other women left the commune?

Paula: When I came back from the Clearing House, I noticed several women were gone. But at that point I was so focused on getting out I didn't pay much attention to who they were. It seemed something really dangerous had gone down and people were panicking.

Amy: What do you think happened that night?

Paula: I don't think Jonah killed Casey – I think someone else did.

Amy: Why do you think that?

Paula: When we were at the ceremony it was obvious to everyone that Jonah was in love with her. He never left her side, he was attentive and kind. But I saw the way Cain looked at her and I didn't like it.

Amy: How was that?

Paula: Cain just kept watching them. He was drinking, we all were. It was a celebration and usually no one drinks at the Haven. But on very special occasions they bring out this wine – it's made on the farm – purely organic. But it's pretty strong. And as the night went on, Cain just kept getting closer and closer to Jonah and Casey. There was something about him that looked dangerous.

Amy: You think Cain knew something?

Paula: Cain was different to the other two brothers. He ran the poultry before Jonah went to prison. He would be quite brutal with the chickens. If they were ill, he'd easily snap their necks.

Amy: But isn't that what farmers do?

Paula: I guess. But he seemed, oh, I don't know, like he enjoyed doing it.

Amy: So, what do you think actually happened that night?

Paula: I think Cain followed Jonah and Casey. It wasn't permitted for Casey to stay in his cabin – that was sexual immorality – maybe Cain was going there to make sure she stayed in the guest house. But I think when he got there, he discovered who she really was. I think he was the one who snapped. I think he was the one who killed Casey.

Amy: And Jonah covered it up? Jonah took the rap?

Paula: Yes. That's what I think happened.

I stop the recording and think about Mercedes' theory. Cain was the eldest, the next in line to inherit the Haven and become the spiritual leader. If they had convinced Jonah that his relationship with Casey was death in the eyes of God, then the only way to save his immortal soul was to 'give up his life', metaphorically. I nod to myself – it does seem to make sense. Clearly, there is no punishment for Cain for the brutal murder of Casey as he is fulfilling scripture – he put her to death. But as for Jonah, his punishment would be to accept 'life imprisonment'. It seems more logical than anything else so far.

But Charlie says I need proof – that I can't legally present theories that name other people as suspects. I decide I need to speak to the lawyers about what exactly I can do.

CHAPTER 10
THE STORY SO FAR

Over the next few days I pore over the transcripts, the recordings, the old case file. I know that there is something, one tiny thing, that will help me unravel the mystery and point to Cain. I'm now convinced that he is the real murderer. Despite still being fixated on the case, I'm actually enjoying the break from the studio. The weather is beautiful and I'm taking long walks on the beach, always thinking about Jonah and the murder, of course. Charlie had accused me of being too emotional, and as I walk I think about whether that's true. I'm certainly passionate – I believe in justice. But am I too emotionally invested in this case? Is this about me trying to right some wrongs?

On Wednesday I tune into the station. I'm interested to see

what Sarah and Charlie will have put together for the show.

'Hi, this is Sarah Sutton and I'm filling in for our usual host, Amy Rhinehart, as she takes a well-deserved break this week. You're listening to *Strange Crime*, a live broadcast and podcast on Radio Western every Wednesday at 5 p.m. Season One is called *Double Lives* and examines the Jonah Scott murder of Casey Williams. This is Episode Five, "The Story So Far", where I'm going to take you back and recap what we know. Don't forget to check out the additional notes and information we upload weekly at Strange Crime Double Lives dot com.

'Jonah Scott sits in a prison cell in a maximum security prison for the brutal murder of his girlfriend, Casey Williams. He confessed and he pleaded guilty. The question this poses is, why? We listened to the investigating officer, Detective Tompkins, tell us that there was an actual defence for the crime committed by Jonah: "the transsexual advance defence" – this would have meant that only one juror needed to believe it and Jonah wouldn't have been convicted for murder and sentenced to life imprisonment. I'm taking your calls, or drop me a line and tell me your thoughts about Jonah refusing his right to trial.'

Having callers live on air is always a risky move, even when Charlie vets them first. Sometimes what callers initially say they want to mention turns out to be vastly different. I hope Sarah is able to think quickly on her feet.

'Welcome back. I've got Ted on the line. What are you thinking about Jonah's decision not to defend himself?'

'The boy's a bloody moron,' Ted says. 'Why would you not try and get off, even if you did it? It's all them video games and too much television. Everyone wants to be a superhero –'

Sarah cuts in.

'Thanks, Ted. We just need to hear from Carol now. Hey, Carol, what do you think?'

'The boy should be locked up for life. I mean, seriously, when does life mean twenty-odd years? That's just twenty-odd years. He should live there until he dies. What he did to that poor girl, boy, whatever –'

Sarah jumps in again quickly.

'Right, it seems we've dropped out there. So, back to the summary. Jonah's motive for killing Casey was that he didn't know she was a transgender woman and that she lied to him and deceived him. Jonah maintains that they'd never had sexual relations. We spoke to Nellie, Casey's former housemate, and also an escort where Casey used to work, about the relationship between Jonah and Casey.'

I smash my hand on my desk. Bloody Sarah. I could murder her. She has dropped her little grenade in at the first opportunity. I'm so furious that I punch the station's number into my phone. But, of course, I can't get through, the lines are jammed. I'm still listening to Sarah combating the incoming calls.

'Hi, Dean, what did you want to say?' Sarah asks.

'Hi, Sarah. I've been an avid listener since day one, I love the show. But I don't recall anywhere in the first four episodes it being mentioned that Casey was an escort. Have I missed something?'

'No – you're right, Dean. We failed to mention earlier that we learnt Casey had worked for some time as an escort,' Sarah says.

'Oh, right.' Dean sounds confused. 'So, why are you mentioning it now? Shouldn't that have been something we knew about earlier?'

'The decision was made by us not to colour the audience's perception of Casey,' Sarah says.

'Yeah, right.' Dean sounds annoyed. 'But you guys are trying to present yourselves as investigative journalists, this sounds a bit more like fake news.'

'Thanks for the input,' Sarah says. 'I'm taking a call from Stuart now. Hi, Stuart.'

'Yeah, hi … look, I agree with the last caller,' Stuart says. 'You have just shown us how contrived your storytelling is. I mean, what else have you left out? I was a real fan, but the last episode wasn't as explosive as promised and now we hear that you withhold information to suit your story.'

'Yes, good point,' Sarah says. 'Thanks for the feedback. I'm going to shut down the call line as I need to finish the summary of the story so far.'

***

I finally get through to Charlie. 'What the fuck was she thinking?' I snap.

'It was a bad call,' Charlie concedes. 'We just watched the listener numbers go down. The text line has gone off the charts. All the same stuff, fake news and that kind of thing.'

'She's just jeopardised our integrity,' I say. 'For what?'

'Yeah,' Charlie says. 'Look, she's pretty upset. Call it a rookie move?'

'How am I supposed to get this back now, Charlie?' I say. 'I'm not even sure I want her on the project anymore. I feel betrayed by her.'

'Look, I know that's your initial reaction, but you need to think this through. Sarah knows this case as well as you do. Pulling her off would be a bad idea. Take your time and calm down. Give it more thought, okay?'

'Okay.' I'm so angry. 'I think I want another week off,' I say suddenly. 'There's stuff I want to do. Next week there's a public holiday – can we put the audience on notice that we won't be releasing Episode Six until after then?'

'Not a bad idea,' Charlie says. 'We can give them a week's

break – tease out some promo material, stir up a bit of intrigue, hopefully that'll drive the listeners back up.'

'Right,' I say. I know, with absolute certainty, exactly what I have to do now. Something I needed to do long ago. 'I'll be in touch later next week. When I'm back.'

'Where are you going?' Charlie says.

'To see a friend,' I reply.

CHAPTER 11
MICKEY

We meet at a small bakery on Lygon Street in the middle of Melbourne's CBD. It was a favourite haunt of ours. I remember long afternoons, drinking cup after cup of coffee and discussing whatever report we were doing. Everything about our life together was so natural, so easy – up until the very end. I watch Michaela open the door and look straight to our usual table. I wave at her and my heart drops.

'Hey, Michaela.' I stand and we awkwardly hug. She draws back from me and smiles.

'Actually, it's Mickey now,' she says gently. 'I recently had it changed by deed poll.' Mickey, my pet name for her and now her legal name. I feel a mixture of sadness, tinged with anger.

'How are you?' I opt for pleasant – after all, I'm here to make things right, not create more animosity. I can't believe how deep the emotions still run … But that's not actually true. They have always been there, simmering beneath the surface, driving me, dictating my choices in life.

Mickey's dressed for the cool Melbourne weather and shrugs out of her navy wool coat. She sits down and unwraps her woollen scarf, pushing her long blonde hair back. 'You look good,' she says, assessing me in that way she always did. A slight smile, a tiny cock of the head.

'Thanks, so do you,' I say. 'In fact, you look fantastic.'

She smiles. 'Thanks.'

'I've been outrageously busy,' I say.

'I know.' Mickey nods. 'I've been listening. It's so good, Amy – it's the best thing you've ever done. It's the best thing I've heard on the radio in forever. Love the concept.'

I relax and the conversation flows. As always, Mickey's perceptive mind picks up the minute details, points to things I need to go back and revisit. We discuss the intricacies of Jonah's position. I air my view that he's covering up something; Mickey agrees, but thinks it's more about him than anyone else's involvement. We are teetering dangerously close to a conversation that ruined us. I pull back from the discussion quickly. My time with Mickey has been so special; just to be in her presence again, to think with her and talk to her, I don't want it to end in flames, like last time. I steer the conversation to her work, what she's doing.

She's gone into political reporting. It's no surprise, she was always going to end up in that realm – campaigning for the rights of the marginalised and disenfranchised.

It's late. We've finished three coffees and shared a carrot cake. The street lights are on outside and illuminate the shiny wetness of the roads. The traffic has thinned and I watch men and women, women and women, men and men, walking together, or holding hands, linking arms, side-stepping the puddles as they chat and head to their destination, a restaurant, a show, home. I feel the deep ache in my heart. I am so miserably homesick, not for Melbourne, but for my past.

'I wish I could go back in time,' I say softly to her.

'You weren't ready, Amy,' Mickey says gently.

'Maybe I could be now?' I am trying to quell my rising panic. Our time is almost over. Last time I wasn't honest with myself, or her, and despite being a vocal believer in never looking back I realise the inherent untruthfulness of that. All I ever do is look back, searching the past for ways to correct the future. I've built a career on it. I have to say it. I have tears in my eyes. 'I understand it all so much better now.'

'We can't go back.' Mickey laces her fingers through mine, the way she always used to when we'd lie in bed late on a

Saturday morning, arguing over who was going to run down here to get the takeaway.

'Too much has happened. We've hurt each other too much, we've changed too much.'

'But …' I want to tell her that I forgive her. That I got it all wrong. That I know we can make it work. The tears are closing my throat up and I can't speak. I'm paralysed by this sense of loss and grief. This could be it – my last chance to salvage the best thing I ever knew. She squeezes my hand softly.

'I'm seeing someone.' I feel the air rush into me, filling my lungs – of course she's moved on. How would Mickey ever be single?

'Who?' I ask.

'No one you know. Her name is Sophie.'

'What's she like?' I ask, even though this feels masochistic.

'Kind, gentle. You'd like her. I met her two years ago.'

'I fucked up. Big time,' I say through my tears.

'Don't be so hard on yourself,' Mickey says. 'I was asking something too big of you. It was my journey, Amy, you weren't ready to come on it with me.'

I nod, but I feel so miserable. I recall exactly that day when Mickey, she was Michael to me then, told me she wanted to live her life as a woman.

***

I'd met Michael four years earlier, at university, where we were both studying journalism. He was beautiful: long blond hair and impossibly bright-blue eyes. We started dating. I was attracted to his intelligence, his kindness, I loved his gentleness and his humour. He made me feel at ease, comfortable with my place in the world. Michael was my security, without question. There was never a time I could imagine him not being in my life. I thought this was it, for the rest of my life. We were inseparable, and within months we had moved into our loft-style apartment.

I had no idea Michael was struggling with his identity. I was naïve. Back in Perth I had dreamed Melbourne would be this cosmopolitan world, and I wasn't disappointed. I came out of high school in Perth and headed straight across the Nullarbor to Melbourne. Melbourne had opened my eyes wide to the variety, the eclectic lives, the different cultures and experiences I'd never been exposed to before. Everything was so different to the sleeping, laconic town that was Perth. Even though I'd lived in an affluent suburb and gone to a prestigious all-girls school, everything there seemed limited. Limited opportunities, differences, experiences. I savoured the diversity of Melbourne, I relished the aromas, the sense that this was a snapshot of a much bigger world that I wanted to explore. And Michael wanted to explore it with me.

We studied and we worked. He was a barista and I was a waitress at different cafes. We stockpiled our savings. When we graduated in a year's time, we would be off: to Rome, Greece, the Arab Emirates, Italy, Turkey, Egypt. The plan was to have no plan. Just to go where we wanted, do what we could and see everything there was. There was no end date on this; this was going to be the next chapter of our lives.

Then he dropped the bombshell.

That night we'd been out with friends to a Lebanese restaurant that had hookahs. Neither of us normally smoked, but it was as if we were getting travel-ready – the old 'when in Rome'. We had drunk a lot of Lebanese wine. It was like rocket fuel, and we probably smoked the equivalent of a packet of cigarettes. I remember staggering through the streets, laughing, and Michael pulling me up the stairs and us stumbling into bed that night.

'Amy.' Michael laced his fingers through mine and his voice went serious. 'I have to tell you something.'

I remember my heart stopping. I remember thinking that he was going to tell me he had been having an affair. The tobacco and the alcohol swirled in my gut. I knew to brace for the news.

'I want to be a woman,' he said. I thought it was a joke.

'Yeah, right, me too,' I laughed loudly. But he looked at me so intently my nausea was overtaken by fear. 'You can't be serious,' I said. My mind started rattling through the memory reel in my head. Images of my Michael. When had he ever dressed in a feminine way, when had he ever expressed the remotest interest in this? 'When did you decide this?'

'I've always known, Amy,' he said sadly. 'I thought it would go away – especially after I met you. I've tried all my life to repress it, to ignore it, I've felt so much shame. But it's actually you who makes it harder for me to deny who I am. When I look at you and see the way you live your life, I want to live mine like that, too.'

And then the memory reel showed me. Michael, always slightly effeminate; I took it that he was more advanced, more in touch with his feminine side – that made me love him even more. His interest in my clothes, helping me go shopping, buying me lingerie. Sitting outside the changerooms for hours as I tried things on and paraded in front of him. His warm smile as he would tell me how beautiful that was, how well it fitted me, how flattering on my curves. Or, the times he'd shake his head and say, 'Oh, not that one, baby.' How the shop assistants were always in awe of him, his fashion sense, his patience, his display of best-boyfriend material. And I know many of them were jealous that I had the ultimate boyfriend.

In bed he always wanted a cuddle. Where he'd lie there for ages, in the early morning light, running his hands over the curves of my body, murmuring how sensual I was. And times I'd catch him watching me intently when I played tennis, his eyes roaming over me in a way that made me feel adored, not objectified.

I pushed myself up against the headboard and stared at him, like I'd never seen him before.

'Are you gay?' I asked, shaking my head. He was derailing everything I understood about people, and love. Our sex life had been full, adventurous, satisfying. I'd never doubted his interest and passion for me. Had that all been a lie? Had he been faking it? Sheer disbelief grabbed hold of me. I felt my entire life was shattering around me into tiny disconnected pieces that would never come back together.

'No,' Michael said softly. 'I wondered that too, before I met you. I went to gay clubs but I wasn't interested in men. And then I met you. I knew I was in love.'

'What about us, then?' I said. 'What about our relationship?'

'I was hoping you'd be with me through it.' Michael was in tears. My heart was breaking for him. His pain was so real. But my heart was also breaking for myself. He reached for me, but I withdrew my hand. His face crumpled and he started to sob. But who was he? If he wasn't the Michael that I knew, then who the hell was he? I felt so much collide within me: pain, fear, betrayal, anger. It overwhelmed me.

'You want me to live my life as a … lesbian?' I spat the word at him. I wanted to hurt him.

'Why do you have to see it like that?' Michael asked

sadly. 'Why can't it just be you living your life with me?'

I got up from the bed and I was totally torn. Sitting there was the man I loved, my life goals and ambitions, my dreams and my future, weeping and asking for my help. That part of me wanted to collapse next to him and hold him and promise him that no matter what, I would be there with him. But that wounded and betrayed part of me, that confused and unaware part, took control and strengthened me when I felt like my world was over. I crossed my arms, I callously shook memories of him out of my head, and I looked down at him.

'I can't do it,' I said, finally. 'I can't be with you if you are not my Michael.'

***

'You felt betrayed by me,' Mickey says now, squeezing my hand. 'While I was feeling betrayed by my body.'

'I did.' I nod.

'I was devastated when you left, Amy,' Mickey says softly. 'I had been so lost, for so long – and yet, with you, I felt safe. But when you couldn't be with me anymore, I didn't know what to do.'

I can't speak. Her pain is so vivid. How did I do this to someone I loved?

'I contemplated suicide.' Mickey shakes her head. 'But I knew I didn't really want to die. I actually wanted to live and I wanted to live my life as me.' Mickey squeezes my hand again. 'So I surrounded myself with people who loved me for who I was.'

'I'm so sorry, Mickey,' I say. The truth brutally reveals itself to me. I wasn't betrayed by Mickey. Mickey had never hidden who she really was. She had given me every part of herself, wholly and unconditionally. I had been betrayed by expectations. I had been betrayed by misunderstanding. I had been betrayed by my own inability to recognise that I loved *who* she was, not *what* she was. There is no going back – Mickey is right. I wasn't there to forgive her, I wanted her to forgive me. *I* needed to forgive me, too. It's time to move on, myself. Will I ever get over her? Probably never. But I guess that's something I'm going to have to live with for the rest of my life. My greatest regret.

'When are you heading back?' Mickey asks me as I wait for a cab.

'Tomorrow,' I say. Despite the pain, this has felt cathartic. All these years I've known we couldn't end the way we did: hostile and in pain. I owed it to both of us. 'You're beautiful,' I say, looking into those wonderful blue eyes.

'So are you.' She hugs me, and this time it's not awkward – it feels as natural as it always did. 'Go get them. I'll be listening,' Mickey says, closing my taxi door.

I sob all the way back to my hotel.

CHAPTER 12
MOVING ON

I'm sitting at my desk, looking out the window. My mind is a mess, a jumble of ideas. Jonah, Casey, Mickey – where do we all fit in? How do we get to live our lives when there is so much hatred and opinion against anyone presenting as different to the norm? There's a knock at my front door. I open it and Sarah is standing on the doorstep. She holds out a cardboard tray with two takeaway coffees.

'Welcome back,' she says sheepishly. 'Can I come in?'

'Of course.' I open the door wider to let her enter. We sit on the balcony and she offers me a croissant.

'Look, Amy,' she says, 'I fucked up. Big time. I'm so sorry.' Her words are the exact ones I said to Mickey just yesterday. And by comparison, Sarah's mistake doesn't even compete with mine.

'It's okay,' I tell her. 'I think you were right. I think we should have released that information earlier, when we first learnt it. It's actually my mistake. I wanted to protect Casey.' I know it's because I feel like I never protected Mickey.

'Anyway. I shouldn't have done it.' Sarah still looks crestfallen. 'I killed the ratings.'

'We'll get them back up. We just have to find a way we can suggest other suspects,' I say, ending the apology. It's over, done with, time to move on.

'What does legal say?' Sarah asks.

'Interesting.' I rip the croissant apart. 'They say it's not actually illegal to suggest other suspects, but it's probably unethical to name them.'

'So we could present an alternate scenario without specific names?' Sarah says.

'I guess,' I reply. 'But it's just not the sensation I want to cause. I want to name them.'

'Then we'd better get back to work,' Sarah says. 'There's got to be something.'

***

At five, we tune into the station. Josie Manning is covering my time slot. 'Hi and welcome to Radio Western. Usually at this time, Amy Rhinehart presents *Strange Crime*, an investigation into the murder of Casey Williams by Jonah Scott. Due to the long weekend, we won't be delivering Episode Six, we're going to carry it over to the following week. Our apologies to all listeners who've tuned in for the show. But remember, you can always re-listen to the podcast and read related information, or hey, get onto the chat forum and leave your ideas at Strange Crime Double Lives dot com. Now I've got this sweet little tune to play for you ...'

I turn the volume down and look at Sarah. 'Okay – that buys us a bit more time. Where are we going now?'

'Let's look at what we know,' Sarah says, 'and what we think we know.' She grabs a marker and starts writing on my windows. I grab another one and start adding detail. After an hour we stand back and look at the thought plan we've created. It becomes apparent that we know a lot less than we are speculating.

'One witness,' I say. 'That's all we need, Sarah. One person who must have seen something. Anything.'

'Well, we know who did see something, but none of them are going to talk to us,' Sarah agrees.

'What about those other women? The ones who left the Haven when Mercedes did. What made them run – what had they seen?'

'More importantly, how can we find them?' Sarah says.

***

My mobile rings, it's Charlie.

'Hi,' she says, 'have you checked out the website?'

'No,' I say, opening my browser.

'There's a storm happening. Check it out,' Charlie says.

The first comment is called 'The Disappearance of Episode Six'.

Strange Crime fans are going mad with the delay of Episode Six due to a long weekend. I've created this post to allow the 1.5 million fans an opportunity to discuss the case so far and volunteer their opinions. The second part of Episode Four was pulled off air due to legal ramifications and now there has been a noticeable two-week delay, as firstly we were told that the host was having a well-deserved break and then this week, as we all eagerly sit on the edge of our seats, we are told – at the last minute – of the scheduling delay. What's going on?

—

I think it has to do with that former cult member. It appears that whatever she said was going to incriminate someone else in the cult.

—

Like the brothers? Anyone else here with me on this?

—

I think Casey was murdered by the brothers and the father. There is something too sinister about them.

—

I was once a member of that cult, I escaped from it too. There is something about that eldest brother, Cain, who is scary.

—

When I belonged to that cult, I feared him too. Something about him not quite right.

'You're kidding me,' I say skimming the comments. 'We've suddenly got all these cult members popping up over the place?'

'Yeah, hang on. I'll phone Will – let's see if he can pull up contacts – you had to register to comment.'

I sit, waiting while Sarah talks to Will, then my phone rings again. Charlie.

'Hey, we've got several phone calls from people who were there that night – former cult members. They want to talk.'

'This is unbelievable,' I say.

'I know, but be careful,' Charlie warns. 'You need to find out if they're legitimate. This phenomenon, the show you've created, has the appeal of attracting people who just want to get their fifteen minutes of fame.'

'Sure, of course.' I look at Sarah. 'It looks like we've got some new leads to follow.'

***

It's time to pay Jonah another visit. Through all these interviews his voice remains silent. He's agreed to talk to me – but I'm not sure how much he's prepared to tell me. Sarah and I wait to get called in. There are a few women here, some with babies, waiting to go in to visit their inmate. I've only done this a few times, I wonder what it must be like for this to be part of your weekly routine. I wonder how hard it is for these women who have to wait, sometimes years, for their husband, partner, brother or son to be released. I wonder if Jonah is ever visited by his family. He's seated behind the glass partition.

'Hey,' I say, 'how are you?'

'Good.' He smiles, and he does look good. He's filled out even more – and he has a lot more colour in his face. 'I got put on the gardening team. I'm outside most days, growing vegetables and stuff.'

I feel a real sense of excitement for him – a small sense of freedom. But then I check myself. I always work from the position of his innocence. If he really is guilty – as he says he is – then should he be allowed this freedom? This pleasure? It's difficult to keep my feelings in check.

'What else do you get up to in here?' I wave my hand around the room.

'Straightforward routine,' Jonah says. 'Let out at seven,

locked in again at quarter to twelve, out at one-fifteen, locked up by six-fifteen.'

'What do you do with your time after that?' I ask.

'Read,' Jonah says. 'Mostly the Bible. I keep my studies up. The only thing is it's different studying alone.'

'How do you mean?' I ask.

'I don't make sense of it like I used to.' Jonah looks confused. 'I read back passages I once knew verbatim and I can read them differently now.'

I nod. He's clearly experiencing the difference between being told what to think and thinking for himself.

'I find it really fascinating,' Jonah says. 'It's like a different book to me now.'

'Do you have many visitors?' I ask.

'Not really,' Jonah says.

'Does your family come?' I ask. He shakes his head.

'"If your brother sins against you, go tell him his fault, between you and him alone. If he listens to you, you have gained your brother. But if he does not listen, take one or two others along with you, that every charge may be established by the evidence of one or two witnesses. If he refuses to listen to them, tell it to the church. And if he refuses to listen even to the church, let him be to you as a Gentile and a tax collector."'

'They've put you out of the community?' Sarah speaks for the first time.

Jonah looks away, he appears upset. There is an uncomfortable silence.

'The show's doing really well,' I tell him, to break the silence. 'The numbers are near two million – it's the biggest downloaded podcast in history,' I say.

'Really? That's good,' Jonah says. 'Why'd you think that is? They don't let us access it in here.'

'People are always interested in murder stories, particularly those involving a cult,' I say cautiously.

'You think it was a cult?' Jonah looks shocked.

'You don't?' I ask gently.

'No.' Jonah laughs at the idea of it. 'It was my home, my family.'

'What about the re-education program at the Clearing House?' I say.

'What about it?' Jonah asks. He crosses his arms.

'Do you not think that it was a form of brainwashing?' I ask.

'No. I had transgressed. It was their job to bring me back to spiritual living,' Jonah says.

I look at Sarah.

'What do you mean?' I ask. 'Did you know Casey was transgender?'

'I've told you this before, Amy,' Jonah's tone is now curt. 'I didn't know she was trans, until I felt what I shouldn't. I snapped and killed her. End of.'

160

I'm surprised by his tone, I've never heard that in his voice before. I feel like I'm pushing him too far.

'Okay, okay.' I hold my hands up. 'It's just the whole transgender thing, you know. It's probably quite confrontational for some people.'

Jonah narrows his eyes at me, he's still defensive, but I see I haven't quite lost his co-operation. 'What would you know about it?'

I realise I'm going to have to give him something if I can ever hope that he opens up to me, at least about his feelings for Casey. 'My boyfriend transitioned to a woman,' I say. I notice the startled look on Sarah's face. It's not something I've ever said aloud.

'Really?' Jonah is interested. 'What happened?'

'I'm embarrassed now to admit it,' I say, because truthfully, I still am. 'But I couldn't do it. I couldn't stay. I didn't understand it. I felt it would change my identity, when he changed his.' Jonah's nodding now.

'I guess I can see that,' he says. 'I mean, say, for example, I had known that about Casey. And say I had had sex with her, knowing that. What would that make me?'

'It's complicated when you look at it through such a binary lens,' I say. 'But probably a lot more common than you think.'

'I read that something like two per cent of births are transgender people,' Jonah says, relaxing a bit.

161

'Yeah,' I say, 'I heard that statistic, too. So, what I'm thinking is, it takes a particular type of person who can immediately accept that difference, especially when it challenges your own identity. I still wish I could've been that person.'

The guard is signalling it's the end of the visit, so we have to leave. I wish I could talk longer. I feel like Jonah was close to telling me something.

***

Sarah looks at me as I pull out of the gates. 'I didn't know that,' she says.

'Most people don't,' I reply. 'My behaviour is not something I'm proud of.'

'Have you thought about discussing it on the show?'

'My past?' I say. 'Uh, no.'

'It just seems so relevant that you have your own under-standing. A totally different perspective. I think it could really help.'

I think about this. Do I want my personal life paraded through the airwaves, exactly like I'm doing to Jonah's?

CHAPTER 13

INSIDE THE CULT OF THE BRETHREN OF THE WORD

'Hi, I'm Amy Rhinehart and I'm the presenter of *Strange Crime*, a live broadcast and podcast on Radio Western every Wednesday at 5 p.m. Season One is called *Double Lives* and examines the Jonah Scott murder of Casey Williams. Thanks for hanging in here with us – if you are just tuning in now, we've been on a two-week hiatus. But please, don't think we weren't focused on the case. In fact, over the last two weeks, my assistant Sarah and I have been trawling through the comments left at Strange Crime Double Lives dot com and investigating some very strong leads.

'In Episode Six, "Inside the Cult of the Brethren of the Word", we are talking to ex-cult members who are going to shed an even greater light on what was going on at the Haven on the night of Casey's murder. To begin with. I'd like to air you some more of the interview we had with Paula back in Episode Four, Part Two. Yeah, I'm talking about the controversial audio that got pulled. Legal now tells me I can air most of this section.'

I play the rest of the interview where Mercedes talks about what she heard in the Clearing House. I'm not allowed to play her 'speculation' that Cain did it.

'So that was from the woman who was present during the re-education program. Is it just me, or did you also find that practice totally creepy? We know from that witness account that Jonah did indeed admit to having sex with Casey. Which brings me back to the same old point – sorry if I keep harping on. So … why lie about it? Why say you panicked and killed her? I know this looks bad for Jonah – because if it wasn't panic, then it was premeditated and Jonah is indeed that cold-blooded killer he was described as in the media. But, you know, I still don't buy it.

'Now, thanks to everyone who contributed to the chat forum last week. Your thoughts and comments created some new leads and new directions for us. We received a phone call from a woman who wishes to remain anonymous. Again, for her protection we have disguised her voice and changed her name. This ex-cult member we are going to call Tanya. Sarah and I meet Tanya in a secluded bar in the city. Tanya is waiting for us and, you guessed it, she's in disguise. I'm pretty sure that her hair is a wig, and she leaves her sunglasses on.

Amy: Thanks for agreeing to meet with us. Now, if I can confirm, you were a member of the Brethren of the Word for something like three years?

Tanya: Something like that.

Amy: And you left the cult in the days following Casey's murder?

Tanya: Yes, that's right.

Amy: We'd like to take you back to that night – can you tell me when you realised something was wrong?

Tanya: Yes. The ceremony – Jacob's marriage – was done and the festivities were happening around the bonfire. These are really big evenings for us – for the most part we live a relatively frugal life. We work ten-hour days, mostly physical labour and scripture study. We eat sparingly. The food is good but there is never an overindulgence. 'Have you found honey? Eat only what you need. That you not have it in excess and vomit it.'

Amy: I'm assuming that's scripture? So how do you correlate this quote and way of thinking with a big, festive occasion?

Tanya: At times like those, when it was a memorial celebration for the community, we adhered to Isaiah 56:12: 'Come, they say, let us get wine and let us drink heavily of strong drink. And tomorrow will be like today, only more so'.

Amy: So, there was a scripture to support every action at the Haven?

Tanya: Yes, but the next day was not the same.

Amy: What do you remember of that night?

Tanya: It was wonderful. What you have to know is that the people in the community loved and cared for each other. We were like a family. So, we danced and celebrated the love.

Amy: Despite the fact that this was Jacob's fourth wife?

Tanya: Yes. It was an accepted practice.

Amy: No doubt steeped in scripture?

Tanya: That's correct. So, the night was wonderful. It was lovely to see Jonah looking so happy, he was often withdrawn, less social than the other brothers. He'd brought his girlfriend down for the celebration and you could see he was enjoying showing her off. Then Cain said to me, 'Do you think her shoulders look a bit broad?'

166

Amy: And what did you say?

Tanya: Well, I looked at her physique – she was a very trim, slight girl and I did think her shoulders were a bit wider. 'Maybe she's a swimmer?' I suggested to Cain … you know, she had that sort of look about her, once you noticed.

Amy: What did Cain do?

Tanya: He spent the rest of the evening forcing his way into their conversation. I could see he was becoming a bit belligerent and Jonah didn't like the way he was talking to Casey. Cain was being a bit disrespectful.

Amy: Like how?

Tanya: Making suggestive comments, saying 'a girl like you', that sort of thing.

Amy: What do you think he meant by that?

Tanya: I thought he was suggesting she might have had a promiscuous past.

Amy: And that type of behaviour is not tolerated – unless you've got four wives?

Tanya: Well, yeah. So, it was coming to the end of the night and I was in my cabin. I'd had a bit to drink. I fell asleep quickly. But a while later I was woken by what I thought was a scream.

Amy: A scream?

Tanya: Yes, it's very quiet at night, so noise travels. I woke to the scream and looked out my window. My cabin is the closest one to Jonah's. Through the trees I could see torch lights.

Amy: Torches? How many?

Tanya: Three, flashing through the trees, and then they disappeared and it was silent.

Amy: Which direction were these torches headed?

Tanya: I'm not really sure.

Amy: How can you not be sure? Were they heading towards Jonah's cabin, or away from it?

Tanya: It's hard to tell, really. The forest is heavily treed, and the paths are quite winding, there's a lot of shrubbery too. I didn't see the end of the lights so to speak. I just saw them reflecting off the trees and bushes. I was still a bit groggy.

Amy: What did you make of that?

Tanya: Nothing, really. Like I said, I'd had a bit to drink, it could've been a kangaroo – or something like that – being chased off. That happens a lot.

Amy: So, what happened after that?

Tanya: Well, there was a weird atmosphere the next morning. Jonah was gone – we were told that he had taken Casey back to the city and he was attending a discipleship training camp for the next few weeks. Daniel and Cain were extremely busy – in and out – and Jacob had cancelled all scripture teachings, that was the strangest part.

Amy: So, what did you all do?

Tanya: Business as usual. The Haven was a well-oiled machine. But the absence of the Scotts created a feeling of disquiet – something had shifted. And without them around we all began to talk.

Amy: Did you tell anyone what you had seen that night?

Tanya: No. It was when someone said that Cain had mentioned Casey looked like she had an Adam's apple that everything fell into place. I was suddenly sure that had been her, screaming in the forest that night.

Amy: You thought they'd killed her?

Tanya: Yes.

Amy: What did you do?

Tanya: I left, that night. I was terrified.

Amy: Can you tell us what your life has been like since leaving the cult?

Tanya: Scared, paranoid. After her body was discovered, I was sure my thoughts were right. I've changed my name, I basically live in fear.

Amy: You believe someone else did it.

Tanya: Yes, I'm convinced of it.

I look up to see Charlie rapping on the glass window. She wants to make sure I'm not playing the rest of the interview, where Tanya names Cain as her biggest suspect. I nod my head. I learnt my lesson last time.

'So, there you have two eyewitness accounts from two different cult members. Tanya tells us that night she saw three torches – are you with me on this? If it was indeed the scream of Casey being murdered, then there were at least three people present – at least three with torches.

'Now, both cult members' stories appear credible and they both are clearly living in fear of reprisal, should they be discovered by the cult. They both paint very frightening pictures of strange and bizarre practices. But, you know, I guess I feel obliged to point this out – why now? Why have these women remained silent until this time? Can we really believe that their stories are true and accurate recollections of a night, oh, what, over two years ago? How have their recollections been shaped by this program? Airing the information might have jogged memory, but you know, could it have created memories? I'll leave you with that thought. Until next week, ciao.'

CHAPTER 14
THE COVENANT

Sarah and I sit across from the lawyer, Lisa Ewans. We're in her office at the Department of Prosecutions. It's small and cramped; behind her is a bookshelf packed with case law, and on her desk are teetering piles of manila folders. She's a small and brisk woman, and her greying hair is worn loosely on her head. She talks as though she knows there's little time to be had.

'I presented the prosecution case at the court mention,' she says, after exchanging pleasantries. I feel like we're off and running.

'What did you make of the case?' I ask.

'It was unusual.' She nods as the receptionist brings us all coffee. 'Sugar?' We both shake our heads and watch her quickly tip three packets into hers. 'The defendant was pleading guilty, so all we had to do was express our opinion to the judge. It was a very quick case for such a serious offence.'

'Did Jonah ever receive any legal advice?' I ask.

'Initially, I believe he was advised by a lawyer,' Lisa says. 'Retained by his father.'

'Do you know what that advice was?' I ask.

'Yes, Jonah told me, she advised him to plead guilty.' Lisa nods. 'We all thought that was strange. I've never known a defence lawyer to cut themselves out of billed time so quickly.' She laughs.

'Would we be able to get her name?' I ask.

'It won't do you any good,' Lisa says. 'Jonah's lawyer died a year ago.'

'How?' I ask. Something sinister, no doubt.

'She had a long-term illness. Died from complications. She didn't have a very good case history. There had been a few issues raised over previous cases. She'd been investigated several times for negligence, that type of thing.'

'Why would someone with all that money retain an incompetent lawyer?' I ask.

'Beats me,' Lisa says. 'So that was what he was advised to do. He did. We asked for life. He got it. Case closed.'

'Would there be any grounds for a retrial?' I ask. 'If, say, another suspect was found?'

She shakes her head immediately. 'It would be very difficult to have a plea of guilty set aside because the Court always asks a number of questions to make sure that the plea was freely, knowingly and understandingly made.'

'So once you plead, despite saying there's no coercion, you can't recant?' I ask.

'Not really,' Lisa replies. 'The best thing would be to lodge an appeal – but in a case like this, I'm not sure what you could appeal against. The judge acted within the constraints of law.'

'I see,' I say. I'm not even sure what compelled me to request this interview – Jonah has made no sign that he'd ever budge from his guilty plea. I feel like I'm grasping at straws.

'There is one thing,' Lisa adds. 'For a guilty plea, you would expect some sort of discount.'

'And Jonah didn't get one,' I say. 'He was given the full sentence.'

'Well, technically, you could argue he wasn't given a non-parole period. So, with good behaviour and that sort of thing, there's always the possibility of an earlier release on parole. Which' – she drains the last of her coffee – 'if you did appeal, he might get hit with. Appealing always involves the risk of a greater sentence being imposed.'

'I see,' I say. Lisa's looking at her monitor now. I know that we've had our allotment of her time.

***

Sarah and I walk along the road in the middle of the city centre. 'That was a waste of time,' I say.

'I guess,' Sarah replies. 'But if Jonah isn't interested in getting out of prison, no one can help him anyway.'

'I think I just wanted to know that if, say, we uncovered something, he'd at least have a chance of a retrial.'

'You mean, uncovered someone?' Sarah says. I nod.

***

Back at my place, Sarah and I are going through the structure of the seventh episode when my mobile rings. I answer it to hear, 'This is a telephone call being made from Casuarina Maximum Security Prison. This call is being recorded and may be monitored. It is unlawful for the person making this call to ask for the call to be diverted or to be placed in a conference call. If you do not wish to receive this call, hang up your phone now.' I accept the call. I'd asked Jonah early if I could be placed on his call list, and he'd agreed, although he'd never rung me before.

'Hey, Amy,' Jonah says.

'Hey,' I say. 'Everything okay?' His voice sounds deflated.

'Yeah,' he says, 'I've been thinking a lot since you were last here.' Sarah squishes up next to me, I turn up the phone's volume.

'Yes,' I say.

'You know, I believe in God, and I believe that sex between a man and another man is an abomination, punishable by death.'

'Yes,' I reply. I don't want to comment, I only want him to speak, but I don't want him thinking that I've dropped off the line.

'And I've been reading a lot in here and praying to the Lord,' Jonah says.

'Yes,' I say.

'And I've been looking at Colossians, are you familiar with it, Amy?'

'Not really,' I say. I look at Sarah – she's nodding her head and flicking through her heavily tagged Bible, a book she's carried with her since we went to the Haven.

'Paul says – and I'm just summarising, apologies,' continues Jonah, 'that through Christ, God forgave our sins – having cancelled the written code, he took it away and nailed it to the cross.'

I'm a bit confused here, but Sarah is nodding her head. 'Do you see what that means, Amy?' I don't reply. Jonah sounds so weary. 'Leviticus forms the heart of the debate on "unnatural" behaviour, on "abomination" in the eyes of the Lord. But when the Council of Jerusalem met in 49AD they decided that the Old Law did not apply to Christians, that it was central to the Israelites' cultural identity. Hebrews 8:13 states the old covenant is obsolete. And while Leviticus prohibits male same-sex relations, it also prohibits the eating of pork, shrimp, lobster, the planting of two seeds in the same field, wearing cloth woven from two types of material, cutting the hair on the side of the head. Do you see what I'm saying, Amy? We ate plenty of pork and seafood, we grew corn next to tomatoes, we wore polyester and cotton blend, we all had short hair. Paul says that Christ's death on the cross liberated Christians from the yoke of slavery.'

'What does that mean to you, Jonah?' I ask gently.

'It means I've been living by the wrong covenant,' he says.

***

Sarah and I sit up late into the night discussing what Jonah's phone call means.

'It's his epiphany,' she says.

'What do you mean?' I'm tired and a bit worried. Jonah sounded so dejected. So betrayed.

'He now understands that his life, its teachings from scripture, were cherry-picked by Jacob to use as a form of control,' she says. 'When I turned my back on religion, it was because I came to the same understanding. We're taught God is all-loving, yet we're also taught God is vengeful. I got to the point where I understood the devil – but God was so unpredictable, he was even scarier.'

'Do you think Jonah thinks that way?' I ask.

'I think Jonah is now questioning everything he's ever known,' Sarah says. 'Without influence from Jacob and with as much time as he has, I figure Jonah will now find answers he never knew were there.'

CHAPTER 15
THE SECOND WIFE

'Amy, you need to look at this list.' Sarah hands me a computer printout. I scan it quickly – it contains about fifty names, email addresses and mobiles.

'What's this?' I ask.

'Witnesses,' Sarah says. 'Some are cult members, some family members of cult members. It's like a pandemic – they're everywhere. But this one ...' She taps the paper. Eliza Stewart. 'She's interesting.'

'How so?' I ask.

'She's Cain's second wife. And she wants to talk.'

***

Eliza Stewart was not what I expected of the second wife to the next-in-line leader of a cult. Like you, I thought she would be a diminutive woman, in both stature and personality. The feminist in me had already preconceived the notion that no educated or free-thinking woman of the twenty-first century would subscribe to the barbaric and patriarchal ideology trotted out in the teachings of the Word: the submission and domination of women, as the 'weaker vessels', justified in a tome over two thousand years old. In a world of campaigning for the rights of women, the beliefs of such teachings were clearly redundant. In order to believe, and willingly follow, one would have to negate all sense of self-worth, critical thinking and the overarching value of equality. Surely …?

Eliza Stewart certainly challenged my own free thinking.

She arrived at the studio ten minutes early. She stood an imposing six feet tall, aided by her towering four-inch stilettos. She was dressed in a crisp navy suit that reeked of money, from a high-end designer who made expensive seem like everyday office wear. Her hair was bobbed to just under her chin; her cheekbones were prominent and her brow high. She had a slightly haughty look – like you see on the face of a QC or CEO of a merchant bank – she had the aura of someone who knew what they wanted and had no qualms walking over anything to get to their destination. So, immediately, I was taken aback, my vision of a mousey, long-haired woman with a French braid, dressed in long, billowy-sleeved, pioneer-style apparel fled out the window, followed closely by all of my above-stated preconceived ideas.

'Amy, Sarah.' Eliza extends her hand and crushes mine in that typical CEO power grip. 'Thank you for meeting me.'

'Thank you for meeting us,' I say, and the feeling of being a recalcitrant school girl in front of the modern and progressive headmistress, is uncomfortably undeniable.

'I want to discuss the podcast with you,' she says, leaving her red lip line on the edge of the white teacup Will had brought to her in the conference room. 'I have serious reservations about some of the suggestions you are making.' I look at Sarah. She is making notes, busying herself to avoid Eliza's impenetrable gaze.

'Sure,' I say gauchely.

'We've been following the series at the Haven. I'm sure it's no surprise to you that we have had our lawyers examining it, too.' She nods. 'Whilst at this point there is nothing defamatory, nor slanderous in the material, there is a sense of projected guilt permeating the discussions. Namely aimed at my husband.'

'I think you'll agree he hasn't been named, specifically,' I say, trying to claw back some control of the discussion.

'Specifically, no,' she agrees, 'but the general impression is there and I want to let you know that if that suggestion is made into an allegation by this station, we have lawyers ready to bring about legal action.'

I sit back, impressed. I thought this was going to be a whispered discussion from a wronged wife who had come to support the voices of the other women, those who had seen fit to escape. I had been expecting the brainwashed justifications of polygamous marriage, sexual abuse, violence even. I thought Eliza was here to seek asylum, to expose her husband and the cult – not deliver lightly veiled threats. Before me sat a rottweiler, on a very loose chain.

'It is not our intention to recklessly implicate an innocent person or persons in this discussion,' I say. 'The intention is to discover the truth.'

'Interesting.' Eliza leans forward. 'Then let me ask you, Amy – whose truth is that?'

The truth. The nebulous idea that truth is a concrete and fixed fact, time-stamped and recorded, ready for easy retrieval, like a book from a catalogue in a library. The truth, which always is concealed by the secret.

I sigh. 'The closest thing we can get to a collective truth,' I say.

'But again, Amy,' Eliza continues – I find this habit annoying in people, the constant repetition of a person's name in every question or statement, it feels like a form of control; by naming you, they involve you and secure your engagement, by recognising your presence, they ensure you listen to them carefully and are inclined to agree with their views – 'whose collective truth are you seeking? Is it going to be the word of disgruntled employees? Is it going to be the word of a self-confessed murderer? Or would you like to search beyond that? Would you like to hear the truth from the family? From the people who were there that night? The people who actually saw the truth?'

I'm feeling corralled into a corner that looms with shadows of deception and manipulation, but when you're in the corner, where do you turn?

'Sure,' I say. 'I'd love to hear it.'

'I joined the Brethren as a small child,' Eliza begins. 'My mother and father sought some type of existence beyond the materialistic world of the city. It wasn't a bad childhood, but to a child like me … well, I felt limited by the opportunities it provided. I wanted education, I wanted material things – I craved everything the Haven stood against. I guess, in a lot of ways I was different – much like Jonah's soft and gentle nature was different to his brothers'. But the teachings of the Word are not as barbaric as you think, or as you certainly depict for a willing audience who love to view the world of a separate and distinct community as unnatural. There is a sense of worth: working hard and sharing in a community-minded vision. Despite all of this, I still demanded my freedom, and my parents grudgingly allowed me to board at a private school in the city for my high-school education. It was interesting being in the world I had so longed for. The materialism was shallow, the values were petty. The individualism I thought I wanted and needed was not satisfactory. So, after completing my degree and training, I returned to the Haven, with a new perspective.'

'Can I ask what degree you received?' I ask.

'Law,' Eliza says, 'a Bachelor of Laws, and my practical legal training was at Thurbury.'

I nod, impressed. Thurbury is the top law firm in the city – and of course, the team of lawyers at the Haven waiting to pounce were clearly her henchmen.

'I returned, as I said, with ways and visions to turn the Haven into the multi-million dollar corporation it is today. And I succeeded.' I saw the glint of satisfaction that self-made entrepreneurs have, as if no one else could have devised, executed and accomplished that very same vision. Was Eliza demure? Far from it; she was one of the most self-congratulatory and arrogant people I have ever had the opportunity to meet.

'So,' I say, 'why polygamy?'

I think she sneers at me, she certainly looks down her nose at my question. The look is one of complete rebuke. And, as was its intention, renders me feeling ignorant and naïve.

'Polygamy is the way forward.' She leans across the table – I think of a cobra, flaring its neck, poised to strike. 'It's not some archaic ideology; it is, rather, a progressive movement towards a superior way of life. In a community, any community, there is often a disproportionate number of women to men. This was certainly the case at the Haven. Women outnumber men four to one. With monogamy, the differential becomes significantly greater when the small pool of men marry. Women are left without a mate and childless. If the significant men are given the ability to marry more than one woman, that differential shifts again. More women are able to share in the loving and nurturing relationship of marriage and the reward of motherhood.' I nod, though inwardly I'm confused. How is it that I find her words at odds with her actions and appearance?

'And what of the other men, the insignificant ones?' I ask.

Eliza gives me that pitying stare again. 'Power is everything – why align yourself with someone who can't effect change, control decisions, alter courses? What is the value in that?'

I shake my head. *What about love?* the sixteen-year-old girl in me wants to shout. But I know, in all of this, love is considered an insignificant emotion too.

'Cain was very interested in my return,' Eliza says. 'He made it clear he wanted me as his second wife.'

'And you had no problem … sharing him?' I ask.

'Sharing?' She laughs at me again. 'How do you share something you don't own? Cain wanted to share his life with

187

me, his powerful position. Our marriage put me in line to control a very impressive enterprise. Think about this, how many marriages fail? I think the numbers are half these days. Consider the ability to share domestic chores, as well as marital ones. More marriages would survive in today's society if there were more people alleviating the pressure. It is a far superior model.' I realise that Eliza, despite her progressive mantra, is as much of a zealot as Jacob – why would she be any different?

'What do you make of the women who escaped the Haven after the night of Casey's murder?' I ask.

'What an unusual choice of words.' Eliza looks at me with that unblinking stare. 'Escape implies breaking free from confinement. I can assure you no one was held at the Haven against their will.'

'It's the word the cult ...' I hesitate – I sense discussing the Haven in terms of a cult is not going to get me anywhere, not with this matriarch, at least, 'the word the ex-employees used.'

Eliza nods. 'I heard that on the podcast. It's blatantly untrue. Those women panicked over an event that was not endorsed, nor condoned by the leaders at the Haven. It's a well-documented, scientific fact, that people in groups suffer from mass hysteria, based on perceived threats and rumours.'

'These women have changed their identities,' I say. 'They are living in hiding.'

'From what?' Eliza almost sneers. 'You appear to be

a rational person, Amy. I'm sure you are able to see how ludicrous their fear is. We run a multi-million-dollar company. We work hard and we live very well. I'll also point out that we pay very well too. Way above the level prescribed for casual work. Do you really think an organisation like mine would look for ex-employees – and then, what? Threaten them to make them return? Terrorise them? It's the most ridiculous assumption I've ever heard. You're better than this.'

I feel chastised and a little bit silly, as if I've been exposed as a believer in Flat Earth or moon-landing conspiracies. Eliza has a point: why would they go after them? What employer would? And the minute I think that, I realise what she's done to me. Her language, her choice of words and her focus on the Haven as a corporation has steered me away from thinking of it as a cult.

'The fact is these women are frightened,' I assert.

'Let me tell you something about the people who come to the Haven,' Eliza says. 'They are seeking something. They are looking for answers to help them understand their place in the world. Jacob provides enlightenment to people who are incapable of discerning it for themselves. On top of this, he offers employment and accommodation. It's that simple. Many people find that the Haven is their place, that it helps them define who they are. Some do not. They leave to seek the truth elsewhere. Some of these people are not mentally healthy, they are bound to fall into feelings of paranoia and suspicion. Sometimes that is the reason they are there. We offer hope. We do not offer threats and intimidation; it is completely at odds with our ideology.'

Again, I see the sense in her words. Frank Moore had told me as much – people who find themselves in cults often are looking for someone to show them an existential view. But then I check myself. Eliza is flirting with the notion that the Brethren is actually a cult, but the Haven is a corporation. I have to admit she is razor-sharp and deadly clever.

'So, if I can steer you to that night?' I'm finding her rhetoric somewhat disturbing and challenging. It's like sparring with the world heavyweight champion. I'm struggling to land a blow, while Eliza is raining them all over me.

'Right.' She looks irritated at my attempt to navigate the conversation. 'The ceremony had ended and I went to our cabin. I waited for Cain but he had gone somewhere and I was asleep by the time he returned. His arrival woke me, and when he turned on the light I knew by his appearance something had gone dreadfully wrong.'

I feel a shiver cross my arms; enduring her pontificating might have been worth it after all.

'He sat on the edge of the bed and told me that he'd discovered Jonah in the arms of another man. He told me that Jonah would be put out of the community. That the instructions had been to take Casey back to the city and not return.'

It's so anti-climactic, I try not to sigh.

'How do you explain the screams that were coming from Jonah's cabin, or even the lights that were seen?' I ask. 'One of the ex … employees said she awoke to the screams and then saw the torchlights.'

'It's obvious, isn't it?' Eliza says. 'When Cain found Jonah, he was with his brothers and father. Cain had told them of his suspicions after the ceremony. But you cannot lay false witness against a person without the corroboration of three sisters and brothers. They went down there with the flashlights. They found Jonah in the arms of a man. Jacob ordered his immediate excommunication. When Cain came back to me, to tell me what had happened, that's when the scream was heard. Jonah explained four days later, when he turned up to Jacob's house – arms wide in supplication, hoping for redemption – that the scream had been Casey's when he physically handled her into the car, as he removed her from the Haven. As for your witness,' her tone drips incredulity, 'how convinced is she of the timing? Is she sure she heard the scream before she saw the torches? Most of the community had been drinking; I know some were quite inebriated. How credible is her recollection?'

This conveniently fills a gap. If what Eliza says is indeed true, then Jacob and the brothers were not there when Casey was murdered. They haven't been complicit in anything; they are, in fact, innocent of any wrongdoing. But it all feels too neat. And as for Tanya, Eliza is right, how credible is her recollection? It differs little from Eliza's, except for the uncertainty of which came first – the scream or the torches.

'One could argue that your recollection could be questioned, as much as our witness's,' I say.

'One could.' Eliza nods. 'However, as I don't drink, I'm quite certain of the sequence of events.'

I see it now. Up on the stand as a witness, Eliza's credibility would have wiped the floor with Tanya. Again, that puzzles me – they could have got Jonah off with their support. I still don't understand.

'And so,' I say, 'if Jonah had been excommunicated, why did he go to his father? Why did he agree to the Clearing House? Why did Jacob let him?'

'Oh, Amy.' Eliza sounds disappointed with me, there is a look of real pity on her face. 'Haven't you ever been in love? I don't know if you have children, but the love a parent has for a child is like the love God has for us. You always look for forgiveness – and if a sinner is truly repentant, God forgives, like Jacob did. Jacob didn't want to exile Jonah. When he believed Jonah had taken Casey back to the city and that Jonah was truly repentant, he did what all loving fathers do. He forgave him and showed him the error of his ways.' Eliza is depicting a very different version of the Jacob I have constructed in my mind – the evangelical, fundamentalist preacher who believes in hellfire and eternal damnation.

'So, Jacob was trying to save Jonah's eternal soul?' I ask.

'Of course he was,' Eliza says. 'Jonah needed to admit to his transgressions. We had no idea of the murderous act he'd committed. Jacob would've turned him over to the police immediately. Jonah maintained that Casey had deceived him. Ultimately, that's what Jacob believed, too.'

'So, no one had any idea?' I ask. Eliza has constructed a well-formulated argument. She would be lethal in a court room.

'None whatsoever,' she says.

'Why didn't you defend him?' I ask suddenly. I think Eliza looks nonplussed. I know that I've just asked her the one question she hasn't already prepared a response for.

'Jonah chose Christina,' Eliza says, and I'm sure she sounds a little piqued.

'Why would he choose Christina over you?' I say. 'Surely you would want the gun lawyer over a very ill one? I learnt that Jonah was Christina's last case.' I see the flattery has hit the desired target. Eliza nods.

'Christina was a well-respected member of the law community. With a long track record in criminal law,' Eliza says.

But now I definitely don't believe her. I know that Christina

193

had a blemished record and that a person of Eliza's arrogance and self-belief would definitely have bullied her way into the defence. Surely, Eliza would have thought she was the best person for the job?

'Oh,' I say. 'But you probably would have got him off.'

'No one could have achieved that outcome. Jonah pleaded guilty. There was no defence.'

'Christina told him to plead guilty. Why didn't she – if, as you say, she was a highly respected lawyer – provide him with the transsexual panic defence? If you had been the lawyer, would you have pushed for that defence?' I ask. I'm enjoying the minor levels of discomfort she's displaying.

'I'm not sure what advice Christina gave him, I wasn't present at that meeting,' Eliza says. And I see it. That slight tilt of the head, the flicker of her eye. She is lying. I have no doubt in my mind that Eliza knows every word that was spoken in the lawyer's office. And she knows that I know it. 'I would certainly have furnished him with that information,' she continues. 'But ultimately you can't force someone into a plea – not when Jonah was exposed as a brutal and callous murderer. He knew he had to be punished for his crime.'

'So you have no doubt in your mind that he murdered Casey. He and he alone. Without any accomplice in either disposing of the body or creating an alibi?' I ask because I can't see anything clearly. It still doesn't add up.

'None whatsoever,' Eliza says. 'When the time came, he confessed to all his sins. Except that he knew Casey was transgender.'

'You believe he knew that?' I ask.

'Yes,' Eliza says calmly. 'Why else did he plead guilty?'

CHAPTER 16
WORDS FROM THE BRETHREN

'Hi, I'm Amy Rhinehart and I'm the presenter of *Strange Crime*, a live broadcast and podcast on Radio Western every Wednesday at 5 p.m. Season One is called *Double Lives* and examines the Jonah Scott murder of Casey Williams. We've got some info for you that might challenge what you're thinking about the case and the people in it.

'In Episode Seven, "Words from the Brethren", I'm going to play you some of the interview I had with Eliza Stewart, the second wife of Cain. As you might remember, Cain is the next in line to "inherit" the cult, so you'll understand this makes Eliza a very important person in our investigation. And I'd like to revisit some of the stuff we've looked at previously, but perhaps in a different light. You'll definitely want to stay

197

tuned for this entire episode – after many calls and requests to the Brethren for their perspective, Cain, Jonah's eldest brother and a somewhat elusive character, eventually agreed to an interview. I'll be playing what he said later.

'If I can start with his wife. Eliza Stewart came of her own volition to the studio for an interview and she agreed to my recording it. Let me just give you an idea of who Eliza is. She finished first in her class at law school and worked briefly for Thurbury, before returning to the Haven. In a short period of time, Eliza turned the Haven from a small produce farm to the one we know, which turns over fifteen million dollars per year. By anyone's standards, that's impressive. She is tall, striking looking and highly intelligent. Don't worry if that's not the description you were expecting of a cult member's wife, it wasn't mine, either and it certainly put me off guard. Now I'd like you to listen to her ideas.' I press the audio. Eliza's clear and determined voice comes through the speakers.

'So, if we look at some of the ideas Eliza raises, she questions the credibility of our ex-cult member Tanya. If you'll remember, in Episode Six, we played Tanya's recollection of the night when Casey was murdered. Tanya asserts she woke to a scream and then saw flashlights. If you stay with me on this, that means that there were people present after Casey was murdered. It kind of corroborated our other ex-cult member Paula's recollection of the Clearing House, where she heard Jacob and the two brothers getting Jonah to confess he had blood on his hands.

'But what if, oh, I don't know, Eliza is right? What if Tanya, who admitted she'd been drinking all night, got her timing wrong? Perhaps she was woken by the lights as they came away from Jonah's cabin and not towards it? What if she heard the scream afterwards? That would put Jonah alone with Casey when she was murdered. And if we revisit Paula's interview, she admits that there was never any mention of murder. She even states that she thought they were talking about sexual immorality and that the idea of a murder had never occurred to her until Casey's body was found.

'But you know what? Eliza ends with a statement that's put a really big question mark over my thinking. She believes that Jonah knew Casey was transgender and that's why he pleaded guilty. I don't get it. If we agree with Eliza's thinking, then Jonah was alone, he murdered Casey and disposed of her body. He told his family he had taken her back to the city and pleaded with them that he had no idea that Casey was transgender. So where does that leave us? With an inept lawyer – who didn't offer him a defence, but told him just to cop it? Or was there something more? Eliza wasn't present at the lawyer's office, but I know who was. Next you'll hear a recording from Cain.'

I flick to a music track and look at Sarah.

'What do you think?' I say.

'I don't know.' She shrugs.

We've covered this in the nights leading up to this episode. Where to go with the interviews from the Brethren. They didn't fit into my belief that Jonah had not acted alone, but I didn't need Sarah to point that out to me (again). Our quest was to present the truth – not fake news, coloured by interpretation, desire or beliefs. And I had to concede that Eliza's opinions did make sense – but only if you thought that Jonah had acted alone and there was no other involvement from anyone else. My commitment to the truth made me play the Brethren's side of the story.

'What you are about to hear next is a recording of a call I had with Cain. Now, let me point something out firstly. The reception on the mobile was terrible, and I knew it wouldn't make good audio. Cain was very apologetic about it – we delayed the interview until he had bought a new device locally, which we could talk on. What does that tell you about Cain? He is meticulous, and clearly wanted to express his views on the subject.' I press play.

Amy: Hi, Cain, thank you for agreeing to this call.

Cain: Not a problem.

Amy: We've offered you the opportunity to provide your version of events.

Cain: Yeah, once the podcast went viral, we determined that we should give your listeners an idea of who we are.

Amy: Can you please tell us then?

Cain: We're a family. That's it, basically. Ours is a large family – we invite strangers and lost souls into our home. We embrace them. This is about love.

Amy: Unfortunately, it's not about love. This podcast is about murder.

Cain: A murder that we didn't know about or have any involvement in.

Amy: We heard from your wife Eliza about that night. Would you please give our listeners your recollection of the events?

Cain: It's pretty much like she said. At the ceremony I had my suspicions about Casey –

Amy: Sorry for interrupting, but what do you mean by 'suspicions'?

Cain: Look, Jonah wasn't very savvy when it came to the Other lifestyle.

Amy: By 'Other', you mean life outside of the Haven?

Cain: Yeah. He had been sheltered until he started making the city runs. He was always this quiet and sensitive kid. He cared about animals and people's feelings. I think we always felt that Jonah needed extra care – he needed protection. So, I thought there wasn't something quite right about Casey.

Amy: Did you suspect she was transgender?

Cain: I'm not sure if I thought that straight away. Don't get me wrong, she was a very attractive looking ... girl. But, you know, I've lived a more varied life than Jonah. I've travelled and seen things, there was just something that didn't fit.

Amy: We were told that you made comments like 'a girl like you' and that you said it looked like she had an Adam's apple.

Cain: I think that was much later in the evening. But, yeah, I guess by then I thought there was something masculine about her.

Amy: So you told your brother and father?

Cain: Like I said before, instinctively you want to protect Jonah – he brings those feelings of protection out. I sensed he was in danger, of some kind, I took my brother and father to his cabin to make sure he was safe.

Amy: And what did you find?

Cain: We found him in the car, in a state of undress. We saw that Casey had male body parts.

Amy: I see. What happened next?

Cain: We were all shocked by the sight. Unclean, unholy. I grabbed Casey out of the car.

Amy: You physically touched her?

Cain: Yes. My rage and disgust made me get the danger away from Jonah.

Amy: And Jonah?

Cain: He broke down and wept. He pleaded with us that he had no idea of what Casey was. But my father had already turned his back on him, and my brother and I did the same.

Amy: Why?

Cain: It's not permitted for a man to lie with another man, like with a woman.

Amy: So, what happened next?

Cain: My father told Jonah he had to take Casey away and never come back.

Amy: Jonah was never to come back?

Cain: That's correct.

Amy: How did that make you feel?

Cain: Devastated. Jonah was my brother. I loved him very much. I would never see him again. He was effectively dead to me.

Amy: It seems a little harsh now?

Cain: No. Not at all. It's not for us to forgive the transgressions of man, it's for God.

Amy: But then Jonah came to you all to beg for forgiveness?

Cain: That's right. We could see what looked like true and genuine remorse. We believed his lies.

Amy: What do you mean by lies?

Cain: Lying about taking Casey back to the city. Covering up the murder with his deceit. Lying about her identity.

Amy: What do you mean by that?

Cain: I believe he knew that she was transgender before that moment.

Amy: Why would he lie about that?

Cain: Because he knew the evil in what he'd done. He didn't want to admit it. Look at it now, he had murdered her. She was gone. Why admit to something that no one would ever find out?

Amy: Why not take the transsexual panic defence?

Cain: He agreed to.

Amy: Sorry. If I can just clarify – Jonah agreed to the defence?

Cain: Yes. Christina told him of the precedent and that it would likely downgrade his charges based on unwanted sexual advances.

Amy: I see. This is very interesting information. So, what happened next?

Cain: Christina outlined how the defence would proceed and Jonah was to plead not guilty.

Amy: If I can clarify this, Cain. Christina Hertz advised Jonah to make a not guilty plea.

Cain: That's correct. That's what we believed he'd do.

Amy: So why didn't he?

Cain: It's the one thing I don't know the answer to. We all thought he would. But when he stood up in court and said 'guilty', I think we were more shocked than anyone else in the room.

Amy: Did you ask him why?

[A long pause]

Cain: No.

Amy: Can I ask why?

Cain: I never spoke to my brother again after that.

Amy: You have never visited him in jail?

Cain: No. After Jonah pleaded guilty, as far as we were concerned he had excommunicated himself from the community. We couldn't look upon him again.

Amy: Why is that?

Cain: His admission of guilt meant that he had intentionally murdered Casey. He wouldn't defend himself. In our eyes that was the true admission of his evil.

Amy: You never looked upon it as a true admission of remorse?

Cain: No.

'So, I've got to admit that is a very different version to the Cain we've been told about. The harsh and brutal man who seemed to take pleasure in the snapping of chicken's necks. This Cain sounds a lot like, oh, I don't know, Jonah? Do you hear what I hear? That same deeply founded belief system? That same acquiescence? That same strength of loyalty to family? But still, you know, what is the missing piece of the puzzle?

'By Cain's reckonings, Jonah knew Casey was transgender before he brought her to the Haven. If that's the case, having murdered her, why not plead *not guilty*? Why not use a precedented defence to downgrade the charges? Why still admit to guilty? Please don't get me wrong here. I'm not saying that's what he should have done – but according to the conversations I've had with law enforcement and the legal system, most criminals do this. They use whatever they can to, if not get off, then at least get a downgrade. So why not Jonah? We'll be back after a word from our sponsors.'

I pull my headphones off and look at Sarah.

'Text line is out of control,' she says, her eyes fixed on the monitor. 'There's been a huge swing against Jonah. Lots of

207

people are now saying that he deserves to rot in prison. Many are arguing that we vilified the Brethren in previous episodes. There's a bit of outrage over the "alternative perpetrator" defence we've been presenting.'

I sigh. I still feel no closer to the truth than when I began researching the podcast six months ago. 'It was a line of inquiry,' I say defensively. 'We know something doesn't add up, we just don't know what it is.'

'There is someone who does know,' Sarah says.

'Jonah,' I say, nodding.

CHAPTER 17
THE CONFESSION

I know that all the evidence, never heard in a trial, has been revealed ... and *we* have exposed it. And with that, the desperate crystal of hope that shimmered in the light whenever another cult member came forward or a friend of Casey's was interviewed – that glinted with the possibility that Jonah was taking the rap for someone, covering up for someone, the belief that he hadn't acted alone, that he wasn't the callous and cold-blooded killer he claimed to be – had shattered. I had lost my faith in Jonah's innocence after the interview with Cain, but still, there is this nagging doubt that tugs at my subconscious every night when I'm in bed, the feeling that something still doesn't add up. There is still a strong pull towards something, a secret. I can't help but go over the *why* of this whole matter, again and again.

Why did he cover up the murder, only to instantly confess? He had made peace with his father and brothers, they had accepted him back into the fold. Why did he agree to his attorney's advice to plead not guilty in her office, only to recant on the stand and admit guilt? That's the thing that keeps pushing me to search for the truth. I'm convinced I don't have it; something is still being hidden.

I have to wrap this podcast up, and it's not going to end in a blaze of glory. In fact, if I can be completely honest, I really thought this podcast would catapult me to the lofty heights of award-winning journalism. I saw a retrial, an overturned conviction, a freed man; I saw that through this whole podcast, with its rocket ratings and listener interaction, I would take the golden chalice in journalism – a Walkley award. It was difficult to acknowledge that I had really only dragged innocent people through the murky depths of suspicion and innuendo to reveal exactly the same thing we had known at the start of the podcast – Jonah was a self-confessed, brutal murderer. I needed to meet with him one last time. I needed to hear him one last time, before I wrapped this whole thing up and concluded my podcast with the cold hard facts of the truth, just in case there was something else.

He rings me to chat, as has become his weekly ritual.

'Hey, Amy,' Jonah says, and I'm sure there is something different about his voice. Is it because I'm hearing him differently, now I'm reconciled with the fact that he always acted alone. Am I hearing what everyone else has always heard?

'Hey, Jonah,' I say, 'how are you going?'

'Good, really good,' he says. 'Can I ask you something?'

'Sure,' I say. Although now my sureness is diminished, it doesn't come with the gusto it used to, when I'd hope he'd ask me something so I could open up and reveal something about myself, in order to get him to reveal something about himself: quid pro quo. It's now a more guarded sureness; my image of him is so dramatically altered that I don't want him to know my intimate secrets, which previously I was prepared to trade like marbles or sports cards.

'Your boyfriend,' Jonah asks, 'the one who was transgender. How did you recover from breaking up with him? I guess it felt like, to me, you loved him very much?'

It feels somewhat perverse discussing Michael or Mickey with Jonah. How did I deal with the break-up? Not well, I figure, I left Melbourne, I moved home. But I never felt a murderous rage towards Mickey. I never wanted to send her body to the bottom of the river.

'I threw myself into work,' I say. 'I moved on. I left that part of myself behind, the pain, the betrayal – not from Mickey, but from me. I tried to find other things to occupy my time.'

'And so, you substituted the relationship you had with Mickey to one with work?' Jonah asks.

211

'In a way,' I say. 'Mickey left a huge hole in my life and my existence. She challenged everything I knew about life and love. When she was gone there was a massive void there. I guess some people get depressed, others get violent, I got reinvented.'

'Reinvented,' Jonah says, 'that's great, Amy. That's like a spiritual reawakening. You knew after that time that you could redeem yourself. That you could transform?'

'Yes, I guess,' I say.

'What work did you do that healed this process?' Jonah asks.

'You,' I blurt. 'This podcast was part of that healing process for me. And I guess it was the reason why I chose your case.'

'I'm honoured,' Jonah says softly. 'I hope this has found you some form of redemption. Or forgiveness. Or whatever it is you seek.'

'Can I come in?' I ask. There are so many things I want to ask him. Look him in the eye and get that final secret. I need the ultimate *why*.

'Tomorrow,' he says, 'I'll put you on the register. Is that okay?'

'Sure,' I say, and suddenly my sureness comes back with conviction. 'I look forward to it.'

***

As I get ready to go to the prison it's difficult not to compare myself with Jonah. I had told him about Mickey in order to engender this confidence, to enable him to see us as like-minded souls. But now I know we are so different, set apart by our different actions and different outcomes. How can I look him in the eye now and get the truth from him, when I see him as such a different creature to me? How do I now reconcile my feelings of betrayal – yet again? I had so wanted to believe Jonah was hiding the truth, that he couldn't be the monster he is depicted as. I desperately wanted Jonah's story to redeem my own. But I had got it so very wrong. We weren't the same in our actions.

But what of our thoughts? When I knew of Mickey's true identity, I couldn't cope with the challenge it posed to my own. Was that the same for Jonah? In that second, before it transformed into murderous rage, was Jonah confronted by his own self? Was it that perception that he tried to defend? Or was it purely a homophobic or transphobic reaction?

There is a knock at my front door. I open it expecting to see Sarah with her morning offering; instead, there are two police officers. Their presence makes my heart sink fast. No good can come of two officers on your doorstep. My mind automatically rifles through my contact list, Mum, Dad, even Mickey?

'Hello,' I say.

'Amy Rhinehart?' one of the officers asks. 'I'm Sergeant Wilcock and this is Constable Fernandes. May we come inside?' They don't need to speak to indicate that something has gone horribly wrong. Their mouths, held in identical lines, hovering between a small smile and a grimace, say it all. It is that face you present to someone who you want to sympathise with, but don't know that well.

'Come in,' I say. My knees feel weak, I need to sit down quickly.

They get down to business immediately, as if seeking solace in their officious manner.

'I'm afraid we have to inform you that Jonah Scott took his own life yesterday,' Wilcock says gently.

I close my eyes momentarily.

'Are you all right?' Fernandes asks. 'Shall I make you a cup of tea?'

'Yes, please,' I say. I am awash with so many conflicting feelings. I don't know what to think. Fernandes moves around my kitchen as though he lives there. I listen to the kettle whistle.

'How?' I ask.

'A bedsheet,' Wilcock says. 'He made it into a noose. An officer tried to resuscitate him, but ...' He holds his hands up in the air. In those moments, my mind races through multiple thoughts and images of Jonah hanging in his cell. Guilt rushes to the surface. Did my podcast do this? Have I recklessly endangered someone for entertainment, or, even worse, because of my own desire to heal my past? Why now? When he's agreed to talk to me today? The secrets are chilling – these actions reek of desperation and avoidance. Was what he was going to tell me so reprehensible that even he couldn't face the truth? And why am I the recipient of this information – information only provided to the next of kin?

'Why have you come to tell me?' I say finally.

'You're listed as his only contact,' Craig says. 'There's no one else on his prison records.'

No one else. Why?

'What do I need to do?' I ask.

'The superintendent will be in touch to organisé a meeting with you to discuss procedure,' Wilcock says. 'Are you all right?'

'Yes,' I say.

'Can I call someone for you?'

'No, I'm fine, I'm –' I look up. Sarah is standing on the doorstep with our two takeaway coffees in a cardboard tray. She looks at the two uniformed officers sitting across from me holding their teacups and it's like she's wandered into the Mad Hatter's tea party. I can see it from her perspective, it's totally surreal.

'What's happened?' she asks.

'Jonah,' I say. 'He's suicided.'

Sarah's response is a gentle, 'Oh'.

***

Two days later, Sarah and I meet with the superintendent at Casuarina Prison, Thomas Dixon. He is a tall, grey-haired man with a pleasant smile and an affable nature. We enter the prison through a doorway different to those of the visiting rooms. This could be the reception of any office or school building. Dixon takes us through to his office and he offers us coffee.

'No, thanks.' I shake my head. 'Thanks for meeting with us.'

'It's always protocol, in instances like these,' Thomas says. 'We like to offer our condolences and assist, where possible, with any counselling, or perhaps funeral arrangements.'

'I've got to admit, I don't really know where to start,' I say. 'I hadn't known him long – I was doing a radio show on him.'

'Yes, I listen in. It's very interesting.' Thomas is looking at Jonah's file. 'It's quite unusual. The police have notified the family, but they don't want to be involved in the funeral or anything like that. You were the only two registered visitors and yours was the only phone number he had listed.'

'They had disowned him,' I say. 'But I would've thought now, well, they might put their fanatical ideas aside.'

'You learn a lot about human nature in this business,' Thomas says. 'Jonah was a model prisoner. Always polite, kept out of trouble. Such a shame, really – the whole thing.'

'Did anyone notice a change in his mental health?' I ask. 'Were there any signs?'

'None,' Thomas replies. 'We're always watching out for that. Prison can be a very lonely place, particularly for someone like Jonah.'

'Because of what he did?' I ask. Thomas nods.

'Yes, and the fact that he knew he was guilty.' Thomas waves a hand around. 'That would put him in the minority here. Do you have any idea of how many innocent men are in this prison?'

I shake my head.

'Ninety-nine per cent of them,' Thomas says. 'You can't believe our legal system is so bad that it consistently gets the wrong guy. So Jonah kept to himself. Read the Bible, prayed a lot. I guess there was always the possibility that he'd have ended up with a reduced sentence for good behaviour, had he kept it up.'

'So why do you think he did it?' I ask.

'A lot of people can't handle prison,' Thomas says. 'Losing your freedom is a lot harder than it looks on television. Sometimes people get to a certain point where they can't survive it any longer. We like to think that we are watching for any changes in behaviour, but sometimes these things go unnoticed. Here's the number for the Coronial Counselling – they might be able to help. Other than that, I've got this paperwork and the last of his effects.' I look at the cardboard box, the last traces of Jonah.

'Okay,' I say, hefting it onto my hip. Sarah and I walk out through the doors and get into the car. I feel a sense of numbness. I'm wondering about the level of my responsibility for his death. Did the show cause this? I look at Sarah; she's thinking the same.

'Do you think we're in part to blame?' I ask.

'I don't know,' Sarah says. 'What did we do? You were always maintaining his innocence.'

'The Brethren?' I ask. Perhaps this is the secret. 'Do you think they made him do it?'

'You heard the superintendent – in all these years, Jonah's only ever been visited by us. He only ever called you.'

'Maybe someone on the inside?' I suggest, as I drive away from the prison – for the very last time, I hope.

'You're sounding as paranoid as those ex-cult members,' Sarah says. 'The Brethren's power is not that far-reaching.'

'I know,' I say. 'I just can't understand why he'd do it.'

'I can. Look at his future. Locked up in there until his forties, what world was he going to walk out into? No family, no friends, no job prospects.'

I think about this. When Jonah pleaded guilty and got life imprisonment he knew he was actually getting a death sentence.

***

Back at my place, I sift through the carton containing his belongings. I feel so intrusive, like this is something I shouldn't be going through. I don't know what to do with it. There are the clothes he appeared in court with. A gold crucifix on a chain, a mobile phone, a wallet – feeling like a voyeur, I open it: a ten, a twenty, a photo of him and Casey. I study the photo. She is pressing her face up against his, they are both smiling directly at the camera. I look at his Bible – it's like Sarah's, the pages marked with sticky notes; I flick through it – he has written comments in the margins, passages are highlighted. I sigh – I can't go through it now – I feel so drained. Sarah picks it up and begins reading the annotations. Then I see the long white envelope face-down in the bottom of the box. I pick it up and turn it over.

'Shit,' I say. Sarah looks at me, frowning.

'What?' she says. I hold it up to her and show her the front.

For Amy Rhinehart is written in Jonah's neat hand. Carefully I open the envelope. It's a letter – some five pages or so.

Hi Amy,

You have always offered me friendship, you have always believed the best of me. I know you believe I didn't kill Casey. I know you believe that my story isn't true. And you're right. I lied to you, Amy. I'm sorry. In fact, everything you know about

me is a lie. And now I want to give you my final word –
the truth.

I look up from the letter and at Sarah. 'This is it,' I say. 'His real confession.' I hold the letter up. 'In this he is going to tell me everything that happened that night.'

CHAPTER 18

JONAH SCOTT: IMPRISONED FOR LIFE

'Hi, I'm Amy Rhinehart and I'm the presenter of *Strange Crime*, a live broadcast and podcast on Radio Western every Wednesday at 5 p.m. Season One is called *Double Lives* and examines the Jonah Scott murder of Casey Williams. In Episode Eight we are going behind the razor-wire and the high-tech security as I paint the portrait of "Jonah Scott, Imprisoned for Life".

'As many listeners know, Jonah took his own life last week. It caused me to look at the ethics of this show and, indeed, to ask if we were – or, more specifically, I was – responsible for the state of his mental health that led him to this ultimate act. Trust me, I've done a lot of soul-searching since I heard the news of his death. And I know this is going to polarise many listeners, but I firmly believe anyone's death, that of any innocent person like Casey, or that of a convicted murderer like Jonah, should still be treated with dignity and respect.

'So, I want to take you back with me to the first episode, when we listened to Jonah's first interview, and fill you in on the things I've learnt about Jonah, the man and his crime.'

I press the audio – my hand is shaking. This episode has been by far the hardest one I've had to piece together, after going through all the interviews I've gathered over the last six months. In a way, and this might sound weird, I wanted to create a sort of memorial.

Amy: Jonah, about that night. Are you able to give us some understanding of what was going on in your mind?

Jonah: It is all very vague to me, it's like I blacked out and when I came to I was covered in her blood.

Amy: Before that, you were at a ceremony?

Jonah: Yeah, it had finished and I was walking Casey back to the guest house where she was staying. Unmarried couples aren't allowed to be together – that would be sexual immorality – but I wanted to stop at my cabin first.

Amy: Why was that?

Jonah: Because, look, we aren't allowed to have any sexual relations, of any kind, so I knew in my heart I was breaking the rules. But I kind of justified it that it wasn't actual sex, you know what I mean?

Amy: You mean touching and kissing, that sort of thing?

Jonah: Yeah. I figured I would sort it out with God later. It was pretty stupid, I know. But I actually had a feeling that Casey was the girl for me – so I would end up being married to her and then this would just be, like, in advance. You know?

Amy: I'm not judging you, Jonah.

Jonah: No, but He is. Anyway, I just wanted a little kissing – a little loving time, before Casey had to go to her quarters.

Amy: And so what happened?

Jonah: Well, it's forbidden for an unmarried woman to be in your cabin. So I was bending the rules – I told her to sit in the car. And then we were making out and stuff and I touched her, you know down there. And that's when I felt it.

Amy: Her penis.

Jonah: Well, yeah, I figured that's what it was. I've never touched another man's penis before in my life. It's an abomination in the eyes of the Lord.

Amy: So, what happened?

Jonah: I remember grabbing her out the car and her pleading and then, like I said, the next minute I'm covered in her blood and she's dead.

Amy: I've listened to the police interview – you were a lot more specific than that.

Jonah: I don't really like to talk about it all that much. I killed her and I shouldn't have done that, I had no right to take her life.

Amy speaks softly: 'I've paused the recording. Jonah is very upset. I don't want to push him further on this.'

Okay, can I ask about what you did next?

Jonah: I think I was in a state of shock. I didn't know what to do. There was this big concrete block and so I found a rope and tied it around her. Then I carried her and the block into the river. Where she sank.

Amy: It was your intention to hide the body. Cover up the murder?

Jonah: Yeah. I knew God had seen it. I knew I'd never get away with it.

Amy: And so what happened next?

Jonah: I hid.

Amy: Who from?

Jonah: Everyone. I tried to make myself scarce. I kinda just tried to disappear for a couple of weeks, but I still knew God was watching. And then nothing happened. She wasn't found until much later.

Amy: The police came to the Haven and asked to speak to your father?

Jonah: Yes.

Amy: And he brought them to you?

Jonah: Yes. When they walked in, I knew there was no good lying about it. I knew I had to tell the truth. That's when I admitted to it.

Amy: You said your father told you to do the right thing. When did he say that?

Jonah: I think it might have been then.

Amy: Before you admitted to killing Casey?

Jonah: Um, I'm not sure, it might have been later when he got me a lawyer.

I pause the interview. 'At the time this was one of the things that struck me as odd about Jonah's recollection of the night. How could his father have said that to Jonah before the confession unless he knew of Casey's fate – because it makes no sense later when Jonah was being totally compliant. The other thing that always struck me as odd was Jonah's reluctance to go into the same detail with me that he had gone into with the police. I know, okay, it's gruesome stuff, and I'm sure any killer wouldn't want to go into minute details – unless of course you're as cold-blooded as Jonah has been depicted.

'Over the last few months, I've made several trips to the prison to speak to Jonah. And he also would phone me from the prison. I feel like I got to know him quite well, and so I'd like to share that version of him with you now.

'Deeply religious, Jonah was the youngest son of Jacob Scott, the spiritual leader of the cult, the Brethren. You've listened in and heard ex-cult members talk about the strange practices and beliefs held by the followers of the Word. We've even played for you the fanatical rantings of the spiritual leader himself.

'Many listeners have held the opinion that Jonah never

acted alone. Or even that Jonah was covering for someone else, an individual or others. I've had to present these views with extreme caution to avoid any litigation. From the eyewitness and other interviews, I'd like to piece together for you what we've been told happened that evening.

'We know Jonah and Casey ended up in the car, and Casey was eventually murdered nearby and Jonah disposed of her body. We know that Jonah's "disappearance" was allegedly a two-week stint in the Clearing House – where he was subjected to a form of mental torture. If this is to be believed and we take Paula's word at face value, then Jacob, Daniel and Cain also knew about the murder of Casey. Can we conclude that they were just helping Jonah find a defence? Can we assume that they were not involved in her death but were in fact complicit in her disposal, either by physically assisting or just by helping create the alibi? But I still don't get that. Why brainwash Jonah into believing an alibi, for Jonah not to use it in his defence later? Why throw away the "transsexual panic defence"? Could it be, as has been suggested, that Jonah was resigned to his punishment and thought he deserved all he got?

'Now, I know it seems like I'm creating more questions rather than providing answers, but can you hang in here with me? This is the transcript of a phone call from Jonah several months ago. The words are his, but the voice is not.

Recording: This is a telephone call being made from Casuarina Maximum Security Prison. This call is being recorded and may be monitored. It is unlawful for the person making this call to ask for the call to be diverted or to be placed in a conference call. If you do not wish to receive this call, hang up your phone now.

Amy: Hey, Jonah.

Jonah: Hey. What's happening?

Amy: Oh, you know, working on the next episode.

Jonah: What's it about?

Amy: Where you grew up.

Jonah: The Haven.

Amy: Yeah, what can you tell me about it?

Jonah: It's like a piece of paradise on Earth. It's a place full of love and peace. We all work together to please God.

Amy: Hey, look, I hope this doesn't upset you, but why would you murder someone there?

[A long pause]

Amy: Hey, Jonah, you still there?

Jonah: Yeah, look, Amy, I don't know, right? It wasn't planned. I didn't mean to do it. Shit happens, right?

Amy: Hey, sorry, Jonah.

Jonah: Yeah, okay.

Amy: So, what you been up to?

'So, help me out here. "Shit happens" – what is that? I have to admit that was the first time I ever wondered if Jonah might be the killer he said he was. Later in the call he starts telling me of his Bible studies. That's pretty much all he does in there after lockdown at 6.15 p.m. By anyone's standards, it's an early night.'

I go back to the recording.

Jonah: What do you understand about homosexuality, Amy?

Amy: What do you mean by that – in a religious sense?

Jonah: No – I'm thinking in a biological sense.

Amy: That people are wired differently, I guess.

Jonah: Do you see it as a mental illness, or just, say, a perversion?

Amy: I don't see it as either of them. I think it's just the way some people are.

Jonah: Like Casey.

Amy: Casey was transgender, Jonah, it's different.

Jonah: I don't understand that. We spoke about this before. I don't know what that makes her.

Amy: As far as we know she was a heterosexual woman. She was attracted to you.

Jonah: But does that make me gay? Or, attracted to trans people?

Amy: Can you answer that if you didn't know?

Jonah: But do you think that would make me homosexual?

Amy: I don't know; have you ever been attracted to a man before? Or another woman?

Jonah: I've never been attracted to anyone other than Casey.

'Do you hear what I hear? And I guess this was one of the things that's always made me feel like he couldn't have done it. Here's a young and naïve boy – in love for the first time in his life.

He lives on an isolated and remote farm and exists on a diet of organic food and scripture through the fanatical lens of the Brethren.

'I want you to hear another phone call I received from Jonah more recently. In this one, Jonah has told me that he studies the Bible alone and that he sees it in a very different light now.'

I play the recording of the phone call where Jonah tells me he has discovered Colossians and now realises he was living under an obsolete covenant.

'I've got Frank Moore in the studio with me now. Many of our listeners will remember him from Episode Four. Frank is a leading investigator into cults and also the authority on deprogramming escaped cult members. Welcome back, Frank.'

'Nice to be back,' Frank says.

'Before we address the audio I've just played, when you were here last I asked you whether the Brethren fit the proforma of a cult. What's your opinion now?' I ask.

'It's definitive,' Frank says. 'You found yourself a walking, quacking duck.' We both laugh. 'But seriously, this is a very dangerous cult. Not only are their ideologies potentially lethal, they exert a massive forward force on the cult members.'

'What do you mean by forward force?' I say.

'A force beyond the community. I spoke to your ex-cult members –'

I interrupt. 'Yes, for our listeners, I'd like to add that Frank offered his services free of charge to assist in the deprogramming of both Paula and Tanya.'

'What they did was very brave,' Frank says. 'It's unusual for a cult member to see imminent danger. Usually they're caught up in the middle of something dangerous or illegal before they realise they're in a cult and possibly their life is at risk.'

'So, what did you discover from our cult members?' I ask.

'Initially, they continued to revert to the scripture teachings – when I challenged them on the ideology. But after a time, they came to see the skewed interpretation; at this point it's much easier to point out the flaws in their understanding of the cult.'

'Meaning,' I say, 'you can get them to see that the cult isn't as powerful as it seems?'

'Yes,' Frank says. 'Don't misunderstand me, it's terribly powerful, but only within the geography of the cult. Once outside, and with distance – both mental and physical – the power weakens. Because of dilution.'

'Dilution of the leader's control?' I ask.

'Exactly,' Frank says. 'Listening to Jonah's phone call, the one you just played, demonstrates the concept completely. Without instruction, Jonah was able to exercise freedom of thinking – something he'd been deprived of his whole life. He was then able to view the Bible in terms of how it fitted with his own philosophy – as opposed to that of the Brethren.'

232

'At this point, I'd like to play you one of the last calls I had from Jonah. Again, the words are his, but the voice is not.' I cue the audio and sit back to listen.

Jonah: Hey, Amy, how's the show?

Amy: Going well – we're getting close to the end.

Jonah: I've been thinking about Casey. I thought there was some reason why she was the way she was – some sort of sin. I was looking for something to blame.

Amy: Blame? As in to explain why she was transgender?

Jonah: Yes, I guess I saw it as some sort of defect – some type of punishment.

Amy: I see.

Jonah: But when I re-read John 9:1–5 about true blindness. Forgive me if I only summarise, but when Jesus was asked what had caused a man to be blind from birth – had he sinned, or had his parents – Jesus answered, 'You're asking the wrong questions. You're looking for someone to blame. There is no such cause and effect here. Look instead for what God can do'.

Amy: What does that mean to you?

233

Jonah: It means any birth defect is not the result of sin. We don't think of someone born blind or deaf as sinful, just as I guess being born inside the wrong body isn't sinful. I think Jesus is saying these are natural conditions in an imperfect world. And that we have to look at why God created them that way. Look at how that allows God to let them do things in their life – to touch others.

Amy: You believe God wanted you to learn something through Casey.

Jonah: Yes.

'So, Frank, what do you think about Jonah's reassessment of the scripture he studied from childhood?' I ask.

'It's clear Jonah sees love and compassion in the scripture now. You'll notice that Jonah focuses on the New Testament and not the Old one – this is because it aligns with his ideology. Another thing I notice is that Jonah isn't quoting verbatim – he's paraphrasing – this would have not been permitted in the cult. The practice there would have been to quote the exact words – that allows for a sense of authority,' Frank says. 'Jonah is actually successfully deprogramming himself from the cult's way of thinking.'

'Again, Frank, I'd like to thank you for your time. Before I finish today's episode, I want to let listeners know a few more things about Jonah. When I began the research for this serial I made contact with Jonah, requesting an interview. As you know, I met with him, and his intention was to show the world that he was not a cold-blooded killer. I've received heaps of criticism for still pushing that idea. But you know what? Of the hundreds of minutes of interviews and conversations I've had with Jonah over the last six months or so, only a few hours have made it to air – you've only heard a portion of his voice. More recently, as I was constructing each episode week by week, Jonah's calls to me became more frequent – up until his death, I'd receive a weekly call. I heard a change in Jonah: at first a feeling of abandonment, disowned from all he never knew; betrayal – by Casey, and then later the Brethren, when he finally understood the way he'd been taught scripture; and, finally, acceptance – I think for who he was. In his last call to me he actually sounded light – it sounded like Jonah had found the freedom he was searching for. Which is why it was a huge shock to learn of his death later that week. I'll play you the final words he said to me in that last call.

Jonah: It's clear to me now.

Amy: What's that?

Jonah: I found it in Samuel 16:7, 'But God told Samuel, "Looks aren't everything. Don't be impressed with his looks

and stature. I've already eliminated him". God judges
persons differently than humans do. Men and women look
at the face. God looks into the heart.' Casey was good – God
will see that.

Amy: You think Casey is at peace with God now?

*Jonah: Yes. I thought I had put her into hell, but I haven't.
God sees who she is.*

'So that's it for today's episode. We're wrapping things up in
the Jonah Scott case. Next week I'll present you with Part One
of "The Final Word" – messages from Jonah's final letter to
me, before he died. Tune in and listen to Jonah's voice from
beyond the grave. Ciao.'

CHAPTER 19
THE FINAL WORD

'Hi, I'm Amy Rhinehart and I'm the presenter of *Strange Crime*, a live broadcast and podcast on Radio Western every Wednesday at 5 p.m. Season One is called *Double Lives* and examines the Jonah Scott murder of Casey Williams. Over the last six months, I've sifted through hundreds of documents, listened to court testimony, interviewed many witnesses and visited the crime scene. I've asked people some uncomfortable questions about their sex lives, their drug taking, the relationships they have with friends, family, even God. All the while trying to figure out what motivates someone to commit such a heinous crime.

'In this final episode, I have used the letter Jonah wrote me to give his final word on what actually happened the night Casey

Williams was murdered. I asked Matt Edgers – you may know him from the television series *Heartsborough High*, in which he plays Dean – to be the voice for Jonah. I must advise listeners this episode contains some disturbing and graphic material.'

Hi, Amy. Matt's voice is uncannily like Jonah's; it sends a shiver down my arms. *You have always offered me friendship, you have always believed in the best of me. I know you believe I didn't kill Casey. I know you believe that my story isn't true. And you're right. I lied to you, Amy. I'm sorry. In fact, everything you know about me is a lie. And now I want to give you my final word – the truth.*

I met Casey one night at a friend's house – not a close friend of mine, he was actually a small-time drug dealer. Despite my very clean, Christian upbringing I was still just a kid. Smoking a bit of weed – while I was told I was polluting the temple that the Holy Spirit resided in, my body – didn't seem a massive transgression to me. Casey and I hit it off straight away. She was beautiful, funny and I was totally physically attracted to her. I think it might have been a few days later, I saw her again after that first night. We kissed, but she would never let me touch her, I thought she was just being 'good', I even felt ashamed of my lustful behaviour.

I would look forward to going to the city to do the fresh-produce run. I found my desire to return to the Haven diminishing, with my desire to stay in the city increasing – to be near Casey.

Here is the first lie: I saw her for nearly ten months; it was my secret – none of my family knew. I was, at this point, living my double life, the City Jonah and the Haven Jonah. City Jonah had a lot more fun, drinking, smoking, partying. Haven Jonah would return from the city with a soul full of guilt and try to repent – until my next trip to the city. It was like being two people; it was like living in hell.

After about two months, I wanted to have sex with her. I knew it was wrong – sexual immorality – but when I said I thought I was going to marry her, you must believe me. That was not a lie.

I booked a really expensive hotel room, with a spa bath and views over the city. I had bought expensive champagne and filled the room with long-stemmed red roses. I wanted the night to be special – I wanted it to be perfect. Casey was so beautiful. We danced together for a long time in the middle of the hotel room, my arms around her waist, her head on my shoulder. Later, we sat on the balcony and sipped our wine, watching the sunset over the buildings in the city. Casey told me that she wanted to go back to school. She wanted to get into university and be a veterinarian. I remember being surprised by this life goal.

'Why?' I asked her.

'Because there is nothing judgemental about animals,' she said. 'They give their love unconditionally and that's what I want in life. Unconditional love.'

I dropped to my knees before her and held her hands.

'And that's what I want to give you,' I said, 'my unconditional love.'

She had tears in her eyes. I brushed them away and then we started kissing. I knew when my lips met hers that this was real and true and good. I watched the last of the sun disappear behind the horizon and I knew that God had created all of this. That sun, her and me, and He wanted us to be together. In that one moment I remember feeling the closest I ever had to God – because of the love I felt for Casey.

I led her into the room and began undressing her. We had messed around a bit, before this, but nothing really serious – my religion kept my lust in check, until that point. I believed that it was all okay, I believed that it was ordained by God. But when I tried to take her skirt off, she stopped me and started crying. I didn't know what was wrong but I could see she was scared.

'It's okay,' I said, 'I love you.'

'I don't think you'll love me after this,' she said. I thought she meant I would consider her used – wanton, promiscuous. But I shook my head.

'I love you,' I said. 'Nothing could change that.'

She was shaking as she slid off her clothes. I was kissing her neck, her chest, her breasts and then she took off the rest of her underwear. And that's when I saw her physical body. I was shocked, I had no idea. I took a small step back – she saw me recoil. And she saw my shocked face. I didn't know where to look *or what to do. I certainly didn't know what to say. In my mind I couldn't correlate what I thought was Casey with the person standing before me. She gathered her clothes up off the floor and hid behind them. She was sobbing.*

'I knew it, I knew it,' she cried into her clothes. Then she started weeping. I watched her sit on the edge of the bed, her shoulders heaving, crying because she thought I was repulsed by her. And at that moment all I saw was my beautiful Casey feeling rejected and hurt – she sounded broken-hearted and I couldn't handle that. I snapped out of my shocked state.

I put my arms around her and embraced her. 'I still love you,' I said.

'Are you sure?' she asked, and I nodded.

'Just give me some time,' I said. I know she thought that this was it – we were over. And I'm not sure if that's what I was thinking, too. But it was difficult to link the visual representation of her to the person she was. We left the hotel. I took her to Nellie's house. She gave me a wooden kiss farewell, her hurt and rejection consumed her. Miserably, I headed back to the Haven.

[A pause]

But when I was back at the Haven, all I could do was think about her. I had never had a sexual relationship with anyone before. Kissing Casey had been my first kiss. Touching her had been my first touches. It had all seemed right. But the girl I loved had some of the body parts of a man. For someone like me, with

241

my sheltered life – only knowing life at the Haven, within the community – I had never seen anyone like her. But then again, I had never even seen a naked woman, in pictures or in the flesh. It confused me. I worked hard at the farm, long days where the sun beat down on me. I was looking for a sign – I was hoping that God would show me His will. At night I slept restlessly, my thoughts always on Casey. I wondered where she was, what she was doing, how she was feeling. I couldn't eat, I wanted contact with her, but I stayed away because I didn't know which was the right decision to make.

After a week I fell sick. Feverishly ill. I was ploughing a field when I collapsed in the midday sun. Several of the workers saw me fall, and they gathered me up and took me to my father's cabin. He called in Louisa, the doctor; she told him I was gravely ill, that I need hospitalising, but my father believed I needed prayer. The next few days were a blend of hallucinogenic dreams, iridescent colours that streaked through my vision. I dripped sweat. They had to move me several times a day in order to change the sheets. There was always someone seated nearby, praying or washing me down with a wet cloth.

In my dreams I was visited by an angel. I had never seen anything like him. He was enormous, over nine feet tall. He was so brilliantly luminous that I couldn't look at him – he emanated a fierce heat. He spoke to me in a voice that sounded like a percussion instrument.

'It is said in Corinthians 13.1, if I speak in the tongues of men or of angels, but do not have love, I am only a resounding gong or a clanging cymbal. If I have the gift of prophecy and can fathom all mysteries and all knowledge, and if I have a faith that can move mountains, but do not have love, I am nothing. If I give all I possess to the poor and give over my body to hardship that I may boast, but do not have love, I gain nothing. Love is patient, love is kind. It does not envy, it does not boast, it is not proud. It does not dishonour others, it is not self-seeking, it is not easily angered, it keeps no record of wrongs. Love does not delight in evil but rejoices with the truth.

'And now these three remain: faith, hope and love. But the greatest of these is love.'

I shielded my eyes against the light. 'I don't understand,' I said to the angel. 'What am I to do?'

'It's simple,' the angel responded. 'You are to love.' And then he disappeared. And with him he took the light and I was left in darkness, shivering in the cold gusty wind that blew around me.

That night my fever broke and I came out of my delirium. My cheeks glowed and my eyes were bright. I was filled with an unquenchable thirst. I drank and ate and my health was instantly restored. I became stronger and more determined. I was going back to the city. I was going to Casey. I would fall to my knees before her again. I would beg for her forgiveness. I would offer my unconditional love for eternity. The angel had showed me God's plan. 'Love does not delight in evil but rejoices with the truth.' If I was in love with Casey, then none of it could be evil – it could only be the truth.

I went back to the city. I lay before her, I opened my soul to her, I asked for her forgiveness. And she gave it to me. She was kind, she was tender-hearted and she was forgiving, as God in Christ is. And I knew it was the truth. I took her to a hotel and I made love to her.

I know this would be hard for some people to understand, but, Amy, I think you understand now. I had overcome the idea that Casey was transgender, I knew God didn't make mistakes. I knew he had created her in that way for a purpose. I knew this was absolute love. I knew my sin was my sexual transgression, but I've told you this before – I believed I would square it up with Him later. However, I knew my father and my brothers would not forgive my sexual transgression, and so I knew that Casey and I had to leave. My plan was to marry Casey and then return to the Haven, with her as my wife. I knew my family would have to accept her then. I knew that they would welcome her into our community, once she was my wife. We would be one flesh and my family would honour that.

Over the next eight months I continued my trips back to the city, to be with her. As each week passed, my love for her deepened. I had never felt more fulfilled and complete as I did in those days. I was brimming with earthly and celestial love. I was itching to *leave, to be with her as one, but I knew my father was to marry again, I knew I had to be present for the ceremony. And then, after that, Casey and I would be free to be together.*

Amy, this is where I betrayed Casey the first time. My hubris was so great, my self-importance, my cleverness, that I thought I could trick them into seeing Casey the way I did. As a biologically born girl. I thought they would view her exactly the same way I did. I had already killed Casey when I encouraged her to come to the Haven. I had taken her to the middle of the lion's den.

'Those were the words Jonah left me in his final letter. When we come back, I'd like to play for you the rest of the recording.'

Sarah's standing in the doorway. 'Are you okay?' she asks. I know there is a good chance I won't be able to keep my voice steady for the rest of the episode. I nod.

'The show must go on,' I say.

The ceremony had ended, Matt continues. *It was late, other followers had moved off to their cabins. The bonfire was a pile of smouldering embers. 'Come on,' I said. 'I'll walk you to the guest house.' It was dark through the trees and the ground was uneven, but I was sure-footed, I knew the terrain intimately. 'Why don't we just stop at my place first?'*

'Hey.' Casey looked at me, surprised. 'I don't think that's permitted, mister.'

245

'Just a few minutes.' I squeezed her hand. 'I've been struggling all night to keep my hands off you.'

I knew not to enter my cabin with her, I respected the teachings of the Haven, when I was there at the Haven. But I guess I was looking for loopholes, to justify my lustful desires. My car was from the city, I saw it as a no-man's land, like an embassy in another country. Neutral to the laws of the Haven. I unlocked the door to my car and we slid into the back seat. All I was aware of was the warmth and the touch of her body. I was so engrossed in being with her, that I didn't hear them coming. Then the back door suddenly opened and I was blinded by the light of a torch.

'What the hell . . . ?' I held an arm across my eyes.

'What is this abomination?' Behind the light I heard my brother Cain. In one swift move Cain had Casey out of the car, holding her savagely by her long hair. I leapt from the car, pulling up my pants. My father and Dean had their torches trained on Casey, who was in a state of undress.

'Let her go,' I demanded. But Cain tightened his grip on her hair. Casey whimpered and tried to pull away, but Cain held her harder. She was semi-naked, she was totally exposed. She was terrified. I made forward – and that's when Daniel held me back.

'What is this evil I see before me?' my father said, his voice shaking with emotion. 'You shall not lie with a male as with a

woman; it is an abomination.' He held his hand over his eyes, in tears, his shoulders heaving. Cain turned the torch on me.

'If a man lies with a male as with a woman, both of them have committed an abomination; they shall surely be put to death; their blood is upon them,' Cain snarled angrily, still gripping Casey's hair. Casey cried out.

I struggled in Daniel's grasp and tried to step forward. 'Let her go,' I said. In my hand I gripped a pocket knife, the one I always carried with me around the farm. Cain released her and pushed her across the dirt to me. She fell to her knees. Dust billowed up around her. She tried to shelter behind me.

'The dog returns to his own vomit, the sow to wallow in her mire,' Cain spat.

'Get the abomination out of here,' my father said. 'You have polluted us.'

And then they all turned their backs on me to walk away.

In that moment I knew I had lost my father and lost my brothers. I had lost the Haven. My community, my family. The coldness of isolation and loneliness descended on me heavily. And this is where I betrayed Casey a second time.

'I didn't know.' I panicked. 'I had no idea what was there. She lied to me. She deceived me.' Behind me I was aware of Casey's crying, but my panic was too great for me to stop. 'Please,' I begged, 'tell me what to do.'

My father and brothers turned. I have never seen such

247

disappointment as I did on my father's face. His grief was visible. In that moment I had destroyed him. His teachings and his beliefs had been undermined by my reckless behaviour. I threw myself at his feet. My brothers looked at me with blankness – to them I was already dead. I clutched at my father's legs.

'Please, Father,' I sobbed. 'Please tell me what to do.'

'Your shame is great,' my father said. 'You have committed the ultimate sin in the eyes of the Lord. You have done the wrong thing. It's now time to do the right thing. Take her away from here. Never return.' My father turned his torch and his back on me and left with my two brothers. I lay in the dirt watching them leave, believing I may never find my way back into their love and grace again.

Casey was dressing quickly.

'Why did you say that?' she asked. Her hair was hanging in her face, her eyes were red with weeping, her nose was running, and suddenly I was filled with complete and utter revulsion. I had sacrificed my cleanliness and purity for a vile and deceitful creature. Behind her, in the darkness, loomed the angel of my dreams. But this time I saw who it was. Without my fever and my delirium rose the Beast. I had not been spoken to by an angel of God – I had been deceived by Satan. Rage filled my heart. Casey was a soldier of Satan, sent to devour me – and she nearly had. When I looked at her, I didn't see the girl I'd once loved, I saw the demon sent to destroy me.

In my hand I was clutching the pocket knife, the one I had threatened my own brother with. My flesh and blood. And so, I stabbed her. Again and again. I wasn't killing Casey, I was killing the Devil's minion. And then she fell to the floor and she was crying, 'I'm dying, I'm dying.' I saw the hammer sitting on the concrete block, and I picked it up.

I knew she wasn't dying, she wasn't human. She was a devil. And so I bashed her head in until she was quiet. I was covered in blood, Casey was a crumpled pile on the floor. She didn't even look human. I still believed she wasn't. I saw her corpse as the vessel used by the Devil to lure me in. The temptress. That's when I picked her up, tied her to the block and threw her in the river.'

I pause the recording. 'In his letter, Jonah says he returned to his cabin, still in a state of shock.' My voice is wavering; hearing Matt Edgers deliver Jonah's confession has shaken me. 'He says that he showered and scrubbed his skin so hard he made it bleed. He burnt his clothes in a fire pit out the back and sat in his cabin for three days and three nights praying for God to show him what to do.'

On the third night, God came to me. Matt continues as the voice of Jonah. *He told me I needed to repent. I needed to do whatever it took to find the grace and forgiveness of my family. So I went*

249

to them. I prostrated myself before them, naked and vulnerable. I wept and begged for forgiveness. I told them I had taken Casey back to the city. I vowed I'd never return there. I swore that I would never have contact with her ever again. They took me to the Clearing House.

I knew that this was the only way I could prove myself. Denounce Casey as the Devil's work, confess my sins. I had to maintain, for their forgiveness, that she had deceived me, and in my weakness of flesh I had almost succumbed. I knew I could never tell them the truth. I could never admit that I'd had sexual relations with her. I had to prove to them that she had been the work of Satan. I needed to convince them that I hadn't been watchful and that my adversary, the Devil, had prowled around me, seeking to devour me.

[A pause]

In the Clearing House I believed what they told me. My betrayal of Casey was so complete that I actually believed I had taken her to the city and left her there. I forgot that she was tied to a concrete block on the floor of the river. It was slow and it was punishing, but gradually I could feel them allow me back into the fold. I might have remained on the outer edges for the rest of my life. But after feeling the coldness of isolation, I was happy to be in close proximity.

The days passed and I was able to forget the Casey I had known and loved. My memories of her had been completely replaced with

Satan standing over her, tricking me into believing this was a part of God's plan. Amy, I know this will hurt you, but I never felt any remorse for murdering her. I had transformed her from a girl into a demon. I actually felt I had done the world a favour. My own secret, never to be shared.

But as we know, that's not how things happened. Three months later, Casey's remains were found. When the police turned up at the Haven with their initial inquiries, I was out in the field. I saw them arrive. I watched the blue and white car pull up the driveway. I saw them talking to my father. I left the tractor idling in the field and went to my cabin. I knew they were here for me. I knew I would have to confess and take any attention away from my home. I had jeopardised it once already, I would not bring further shame and disappointment to my father.

I was waiting for them, when they came for me. When the investigating officer asked if I knew anything about the body in the river, I heard my father's voice: 'It's now time to do the right thing.' I knew it was God, speaking through him. And so, I confessed to her murder.

I believed with every fibre of my being that my father and brothers would be more accepting of that transgression than they would my admission of knowing Casey was transgender and having sexual relations with her. I believed I would keep my family, even though I was a murderer. In the beginning, I was right. My father, knowing that she had been the work of the Devil, posted my bail and took me to a lawyer. I could choose Eliza, my brother's second wife – but I knew she would see the truth, I knew I would never get away with what I'd done. Or Christina, who was very frail – and I felt I had a better chance of manipulating her. But it was here I realised how smart the Beast was, the depths of his deception.

'So, it's pretty heavy going, right?' I say into my mike. 'We have the actual events that occurred leading up to Casey's brutal murder, and the subsequent "resetting" of Jonah's thinking. For me, it's difficult to hear all of this, because, I guess, I always wanted to believe he hadn't acted alone. If you listen to what he believes, and you know I do believe this is the truth, then he thought he was up against the workings of evil. So, I'm going to leave this episode here for this week. Next week I'll air Part Two, the last instalment of "The Final Word".'

I take my headphones off. I'm shattered, disappointed, I so wanted this not to end this way. I so desperately wanted Jonah not to be this person. I needed to believe there were people out there, like Jonah, who would accept a person like Casey unconditionally. But like me, he had proven that he couldn't.

CHAPTER 20
THE FINAL WORD: PART TWO

'Hi, I'm Amy Rhinehart and I'm the presenter of *Strange Crime*, a live broadcast and podcast on Radio Western every Wednesday at 5 p.m. Season One is called *Double Lives* and examines the Jonah Scott murder of Casey Williams. This is Part Two of the final episode. It's called "The Final Word" and is based on the letter Jonah left for me after his suicide. If you haven't listened to Part One, I strongly suggest you go back now and do it. A reminder to listeners, we have Matt Edgers – you may know him from *Heartsborough High*, in which he plays Dean – to be the voice for Jonah. I must advise listeners, this episode contains some disturbing and graphic material.

'Part Two of this, the final episode, begins with Jonah telling me about the lawyer his father retains for him.' I flick the audio.

Christina Hertz was a member of the Brethren of the Word and a criminal lawyer. I met her with my father and brothers at her office in the city. It was frightening being back in the city. I had blanked it from my memories, but as our car came off the freeway and started driving down St George's Terrace, the feeling of hostility the place imbued was overwhelming. I felt the windows on the buildings were eyes that could see straight into my soul. And I knew my soul was black.

Christina had an illness, and I was to be the last client she ever represented. We sat in her office and I outlined what had happened. I began with meeting Casey, I omitted any sexual relations from my recall, except the night when my family had found me in the car.

'When I put my hand there, I felt it,' I said.

'Her penis?' Christina asked. I nodded, I noticed my brothers and my father had looked away. I sensed the shame in all of them. 'And then you panicked?'

I said, 'I had been deceived by her. She had told me she was a girl. Well, not actually said it, but pretended to be one. I was a virgin. We hadn't touched each other any more than a few kisses. I had no idea.'

'And you confessed to the police that you had murdered her and disposed of the body?' Christina asked.

I nodded my head. 'I didn't see the point in hiding, I had brought enough shame upon my family. I knew I had to admit it.' I watched my father's body language as he moved slightly away from me.

'There is a defence,' Christina said eventually. 'It's called the transsexual advance defence.'

I felt like God had intervened. There was a defence for my actions. Even the law knew the deception of the Devil could drive good men to evil acts.

'All we need to do is prove that Casey deceived you,' Christina said. 'We'll need witnesses from the city who saw you together. You need to make a list of people who can attest to the time frame and the nature of your relationship. We need to prove that Casey had kept her past a secret, that you had been totally unaware. Once we establish that, we can fight on the grounds of unwanted sexual advances – it has a strong precedent in court.'

My father leaned forward. 'So, Jonah could get off?' he asked.

'Downgraded,' Christina said, 'to manslaughter. You will still go to jail – but for significantly less time. Probably ten years and out in six.'

I couldn't hear what she was saying clearly. All I could hear was laughter, long and loud, like the sound of cymbals and gongs. It was the Devil laughing at me. He was taunting me. 'Defend yourself, Jonah,' he mocked, 'and then they'll know. Everyone will know. You knowingly lay with a man as with a woman. You are the abomination. You have blood on your hands.'

I clutched my head to stop the Devil's laughter, but it wouldn't diminish. And in this transcendental moment my two personas merged into one. City Jonah and Haven Jonah became Jonah the Murderer. There was no way Christina could find anyone to prove that Casey had deceived me – in fact, everyone in the city would prove the opposite. And then I remembered the hotel receipts. There was no way out. If I stood in the court room to defend myself of murder – then everything else, all of my other sins, every other transgression, would be exposed.

But I couldn't say any of this. In Christina's office we worked through the defence. My father softened when we wrote down the deception and the lies Casey had exposed me to. When I explained how I had seen Satan rise behind her, I saw my father nod. I knew he believed me. He saw that I had been tempted into the Devil's work by the Devil himself. So, everyone in that room believed I would plead not guilty at the hearing.

I dressed for court that morning. I felt like Judas. I knew I was going to betray everyone yet again. They were expecting me to stand before the judge and plead not guilty to the crime. But I knew I had no choice. When I looked at myself in the mirror that morning, I knew it would be the last time I would ever be free. I knew I'd never return to the Haven. I knew I'd never be in the fields again. It pained me. But you know what, Amy? I truly believed that by keeping my secret, by not revealing my sexual immorality – the abomination – that I wouldn't be outcast from the Brethren. That was what I was clinging to. I'd take the punishment for killing Casey – but I'd retain my former identity, I wouldn't be outcast into the desert of isolation and loneliness. It was all I had left.

When I stood before the judge and said 'guilty,' I heard the Devil's laughter ringing around me for the last time. I turned to my father and I saw in his eyes he knew what I'd done. He saw every one of my sins. He knew why I'd pleaded guilty. He knew what I was covering up. His eyes locked with mine and they were empty. That was the last time I laid eyes on any member of the Brethren. From that moment on, I was dead to them.

'So,' I say into my mike. 'That was the true confession, and to me I guess it makes sense. You know, that thing that didn't add up? Now we know. He wanted back into the favours of his father and brothers. His brainwashing led him to believe that murder, while wrong in the eyes of the law, was justified in the eyes of the Brethren. We'll hear more from Jonah after the break. Just stay with me.'

***

Charlie comes into the studio with a glass of water. 'You okay?' I nod and take the glass.

'I feel like weeping,' I say. 'It's all so real and so sad now.'

'I know, Amy,' Charlie says. 'We're getting some mixed responses on the text line. It seems there were a lot of people in your camp after all, still defending Jonah, blaming fanatical religious beliefs as the murderer in this case.'

'But we can't defend him anymore,' I say wearily. 'He did it. All of it. On his own.'

'I know.' Charlie gives me a half smile. 'Ten more minutes, kiddo. Then it will all be over.'

***

I flick my mike back on. 'Thanks for staying with me. We've been listening to a recording of the final letter Jonah wrote to me before he took his life. As you know, once abandoned by the Brethren, Jonah sought solace in the Bible. It makes sense to me, right? It's the only way of living life he's ever known. He's looking for redemption and peace, but what does he find instead? I'll leave it to Jonah to tell you.'

The Bible was different to me. Every time I read a passage, the words formed different meanings. I couldn't see it the way I'd been taught – there was no one to explain it to me. For the first time it was an unfamiliar thing, a foreign language to try to decipher. And that's when I discovered the contradictions – it wasn't black and white, it was so many shades in between.

At the Haven we had focused on fear and retribution. Our teachings had been about God's anger and will. By subjugating ourselves and depriving our natural human needs we were proving ourselves worthy of our Maker. But on my own, night after night in my prison cell, I learnt about a different God. A God of forgiveness and understanding. I knew this God wouldn't allow his children to suffer for eternity for sin. I knew this God would take true repentance as goodness of the heart and help heal the soul. This God was absolute Love.

A God of Love would never accept a murderous heart. He would never condone it. He would never see it as the path of the righteous. And it came to me as an epiphany. I had killed a girl. I had killed a girl I had loved with my entire heart. I'd taken away her life. I'd stolen her future. I had thought I was nobly living out my punishment and I had God's forgiveness because I had acted 'pure of heart' by ridding the world of evil.

When I realised what I'd done, I was filled with total and complete revulsion – for myself.

Casey had never been the work of the Devil and I had never carried out the work of the Lord. It was me. I was the minion of Satan. I actually was that cold-blooded killer I had denied being from the beginning.

I was full of hatred and self-loathing. I despised my arrogance, my belief that I was righteous and good. I wasn't good. Casey was.

And then I knew what I had to do. I have to face my Maker. I can't go on living here on Earth. I don't belong. I gave up my right to exist on this earthly plane when I killed a beautiful, warm-blooded, kind soul. I have to face Him now. I have to

humble myself before Him, on my knees, and pray for forgiveness.
I have to believe that my God will see into my heart, will accept
my repentance and will forgive me.

'Those were the final words of Jonah Scott, the 21-year-old murderer of Casey Williams, seventeen. In concluding, I'd like to share with you my final thoughts. When I started this podcast, I was on a quest for truth. I've learnt, much like Jonah learnt about his God, that it's not a black and white journey. Truth is like a lens we apply to everything we see. It is malleable and transformative. We can bend it, mould it, shape it, vanish it. Our minds allow us to foreground parts of it and background others. We do this to present the versions of ourselves we want the world to see, and to hide the versions we can't bear to reveal.

'Let me be honest here, you all know I was a huge supporter of Jonah. When I began investigating his case, I knew there were gaps and silences in the story. Small little spaces, with nuanced language, masking the secret beneath. I wanted to prise the masks off and peer into the dark. I guess I did, right?

'What this story has shown me is the vulnerability of people. How easily we can be affected by words, thoughts and deeds. I believed I was presenting an unbiased account of the Casey Williams murder, but you know what? I guess I didn't. I guess the truth is in every detail I omitted that ended up on the editing room floor, because I was driven by my own personal belief that Jonah hadn't acted alone.

'But he did. Was he a victim? Some may argue that he was as much a victim of fanatical teachings as Casey was a victim of society's prejudices. Some may argue that Jonah entered a delusional state because of the indoctrination he was forced to endure all of his life, like Casey was forced to hide her true identity for fear for her life. No matter how we look at it, this is the truth: Jonah Scott, acting alone, murdered an innocent young girl. And then, to add further ignominy to the crime, he disposed of her body like she was a piece of rubbish. Jonah received life imprisonment, as we know, and some will argue that's not enough. But I want to ask you this. What is enough? When is it enough? Unable to live with his realisation of the true callous and brutal actions he committed, Jonah hanged himself in his prison cell. Some will say that justice has been served. The scales are now even, the ledger now balanced.

'But let's not forget that, at the end of this sorry tale, two young people are both dead, through ignorance, judgement and hatred. I called this the "Final Word" and I allowed Jonah to have it. But he doesn't deserve it, no matter what your position is. So, I want to leave you with Casey. Throughout the entire podcast she has remained voiceless. This is an audio clip her cousin Raquel gave me from one of the videos Casey posted on Facebook before her death. In the vision she is getting dressed to go out. The other voice you will hear is her friend Nellie.' I press the audio and sit back.

Nellie: Hey, girl – where you going?

Casey [giggles]: Out. Out. Out and about.

Nellie: Who with tonight?

Casey: My handsome prince.

Nellie: You think your handsome prince gonna come and save you on his shiny white horse?

Casey: Nellie! I don't need to be saved by a prince.

Nellie: Why's that?

Casey: Because look at me. I've already saved myself.

[Laughter]

I pull my headphones back on and clear my throat. I'd listened to that recording several times before making the decision to play it. Now I hoped it was the right one. I love her sentiment, I love her attitude. I wish I could have met her. I have tears in my eyes. The thing that hurts my heart when I listen to it is her tone. It's the voice of a young girl, with her life ahead of her, one where the possibilities are endless. I clear my throat again and speak, somewhat thickly, into the microphone. 'This ends our serial *Double Lives*, and so I'd like to thank you for hanging in here with me. I'll be back some time next year with another series of *Strange Crime*. I'm Amy Rhinehart. Ciao.'

ACKNOWLEDGEMENTS

The finished book you hold in your hand, is the result of so many people's collective energy. My thanks go to my agent, Fiona Johnson, who worked tirelessly to place this work in the hands of the right publisher. Thanks to Juliet Rogers and Diana Hill of Echo Publishing for your unwavering support and enthusiasm; to my editor, Rochelle Fernandez – I appreciate your eagle eye for detail; and to Erin Kyan, for your insightful feedback. Thanks to Barbara Horgan, who has been a stoic supporter of this work from day one.

I always have to thank the usual suspects, Jane, Savannah, Willow and Nick, for listening to me read the latest instalment, or putting up with me disappearing for hours on end to research and write; many thanks to Uber for the food deliveries.

KATE McCAFFREY

While I am a fiction writer, the events I write of are inspired by the world we live in. As a fan of true crime podcasts, the hugely popular podcast by Sarah Koenig, *Serial: This American Life*, and Hedley Thomas's *The Teacher's Pet*, were inspirational. Having researched extensively for the background setting of this book, and flexing a bit of creative muscle, any omissions or errors are my own.

And finally, I would like to thank the many individuals who shared their stories with me. Thank you for letting me be a part of your journey.

Kate McCaffrey